"You're a cool o...,
Claire Kingston."

Rafe's gravelly voice was low, as heady as heated brandy. "But you're not as cool as you think. You're not as cool as anyone thinks. There's a volcano under that ice. I see it in your eyes every time you look at me. I see it in the way you move your body. I see it right—" he lifted his hand slowly and touched the pulse throbbing above the collar of her silk blouse "—there. One of these days you're going to explode with all the passion that's locked up inside you. All you need is someone to give you a push in the right direction. Someone to light the fuse for you. And I'm going to be that someone."

Dear Reader,

I confess. I'm a movie junkie. The habit started when I was a little kid. I'd spend my allowance on the Saturday matinee and sit through *both* features and the cartoons, at least twice. As an adult, one of my favorite indulgences is to see four or five movies over a weekend, either at the local cinema or cuddled up on the couch in front of my video machine. I'll watch just about any kind of movie—Western, action, science fiction, suspense, drama or, of course, romance.

I've always been equally intrigued with the processes and people who make the movies. I'm an avid reader of *People, Entertainment Weekly,* and *Premiere,* I've read every actor's biography ever written and I found "The Making of *Terminator 2*" as spellbinding as the movie itself.

So, of course, I was *destined* to write about the Kingstons' Hollywood Dynasty.

The research was fascinating! I learned about storyboarding, gaffers, dolly grips, intercutting and the difference between a dissolve and a fade. Research also gave me a guilt-free reason to read all the supermarket tabloids—where I found out that nothing I could dream up for my Hollywood heroes and heroines could come *close* to what's printed about real-life movie stars.

So make yourself a big bowl of popcorn and curl up in your favorite reading spot. I hope you have as much fun reading about living and loving in Hollywood as I did writing about it.

Sincerely,

Candace Schuler

P.S. I love to hear from my readers!

THE RIGHT DIRECTION

CANDACE SCHULER

Harlequin Books

TORONTO • NEW YORK • LONDON
AMSTERDAM • PARIS • SYDNEY • HAMBURG
STOCKHOLM • ATHENS • TOKYO • MILAN
MADRID • WARSAW • BUDAPEST • AUCKLAND

To my dad,
Denzil Darwin Schnabel,
who has a marshmallow heart, too

ISBN 0-373-25567-5

THE RIGHT DIRECTION

1

THE TABLOIDS HAD christened her the Ice Queen of Hollywood and, for once, the tabloids were right on the money, Rafe thought, staring at the face of the woman who looked up at him from the front page of the *National Enquirer*. She was incredibly beautiful—if you went for the cool, touch-me-not, Grace Kelly type of beauty. Which, he reminded himself, he didn't. Her hair was a rich sable brown, pulled back into a low, puffy bun that made a woman with her delicate bone structure look as elegant and ethereal as a prima ballerina. Her eyes were huge and blue, although, he thought uncharitably, certainly not as blue as the picture made them out to be. They were expertly and subtly made-up, fringed with thick dark lashes and framed by perfectly arched brows. Her nose was narrow and aristocratic, tailor-made for looking down, and her skin was as pale and flawless as an alabaster rose. Only her mouth showed any indication that a real woman might be lurking beneath the perfect facade.

It was a delicious cupid's bow of a mouth, with a short upper lip that gave her face the purity of a Victorian cameo and a full lower one that made Rafe think fleetingly of flickering firelight and red silk sheets. But the tight, oh-so-gracious smile curving those tempting lips ruined his little fantasy of sweet, seductive womanhood before it got started. It was a patently false smile, lacking even a semblance of real warmth. The expression in those huge blue eyes was cool, impatient and annoyed, as if she were totally unimpressed with whatever she was looking at. Which was probably the poor working stiff who was only doing his job by taking her picture.

Rafe Santana took one last look at Her Highness exiting Spago on the arm of the very married Don Johnson and tossed the tabloid onto the metal desk next to his booted feet. It skittered across the surface, coming to rest against the untidy pile of old magazines and industry newspapers already there, all of it relating in some way to the beautiful Ms. Claire Kingston. He'd muddled through half of it before he realized it wasn't necessary to read everything to know what kind of woman she was. He was already well acquainted with her type, he thought, his eyes inexorably drawn back to the exquisitely feminine face that looked up at him with such well-bred scorn. She was a princess. A pampered, privileged, Anglo-Saxon princess with impeccable bloodlines and nothing but the purest ice water flowing through her delicate blue veins. Oh, yes, indeed, he knew her type, all right. He'd dealt with women like her before, much to his detriment.

And at four o'clock that afternoon he was scheduled to meet with her to discuss his future.

"What the hell does a woman like that know about making movies?" he grumbled to himself.

"Hmm?" The young woman sitting at the desk in the opposite corner of the room looked up from her computer screen. She was olive skinned, like her employer, with dark glossy hair cut in a short, sophisticated bob and large brown eyes set above slanted cheekbones. She was his youngest sister, the fifth child in a brood of seven. "What did you say?"

Rafe gestured at the tabloid. "Claire Kingston. What the hell does she know about making movies?"

"Quite a lot, apparently," Pilar Santana said. "She's supposed to be one of the hottest young producers in Hollywood."

"Hype," Rafe snorted.

"*Two by Two, All's Fair, The Promise, The Devil's Game, Glory Days*," Pilar said, naming the last five movies Claire Kingston had been involved in. She didn't have to add that they had all done extremely well at the box office, because he knew it as well as she did. "Doesn't sound like hype to me. Sounds like the lady's one sharp, savvy producer."

"*Assistant* producer," Rafe corrected her. "And she probably wouldn't have that title to her credit if it weren't for her illustrious family name."

Pilar grinned. "What? You mean the same way I wouldn't have this job if I weren't related to you?"

He ignored her efforts to tease him out of his sour mood. "Everybody who's anybody in this business knows her mother is the real brains behind Kingston Productions," Rafe told his sister. "Elise Gage is the one who puts the deals together and oversees production.

And if Claire's *mother* isn't directly involved in a given project, then one of her *brothers* is either starring in it or in charge of cinematography. Or her father is directing. Or all four together. As far as I can tell from reading these—" he touched the haphazard pile of magazines with the toe of his boot, inadvertently sending most of them toppling to the floor "—the Ice Queen spends all her time going to parties and premieres. Hell—" he took his booted feet from the desk with a disgruntled snort and bent over to pick up the magazines "—at best, she's just a glorified gofer."

"Aren't you being just a little hard on her?" Pilar argued as he dropped the magazines back onto his desk with a thump. "She could be a very nice, very capable person."

Rafe looked down at Claire Kingston's photograph again, consideringly. She smiled back at him. Cool. Beautiful. Imperious as a royal princess. "I doubt it," he said flatly.

Pilar shook her head. "Well, nice person or not, you'd better find a way to deal with her, because you're going to be working together for some time," she advised sagely. "*If* she decides to hire you to direct *Desperado*."

"Oh, she'll hire me, all right," Rafe murmured as his sister turned her attention back to the computer screen. The softly spoken words carried the force of an incantation. Or a prayer. He'd been interested in the project from the moment the script had been delivered to his office by special messenger. Kingston Productions was a class act and he was flattered to be considered by them so early in his career. Ten minutes into the screenplay his interest had hardened into a steely determination that grew stronger with each line he read. *Desperado* was everything a screenplay should be. Sensitive. Insightful. Powerful. Career making.

And he was going to direct it.

He reached out and touched the printed image of Claire Kingston's mouth with the tip of his index finger, absently tracing the delicate curve of her upper lip as he repeated the silent vow. Nothing was going to stop him from directing *Desperado*, not even a frosty Hollywood socialite who had delusions of being a real producer.

"MORNING, ROBERT," Claire Kingston said as she pushed open the door to her suite of offices on the studio lot. She breezed by her assistant's desk without stopping. "Get Mike Ovitz's office on the phone for me, please," she said, getting right down to business as was her way. "I heard a hot bit of gossip over breakfast this morning that I'd like to check out with him."

"That script Madonna's been shopping around?" Robert asked.

Claire paused with her hand on the doorknob to her office and glanced back at her assistant. "How'd you hear about it already? The rumors only started making the rounds at Hugo's this morning," she said, naming the current Hollywood hot spot for power-breakfasting.

Robert shrugged. "I have my sources."

Claire smiled at him. "I'll bet you do," she said, knowing from experience that the Hollywood grapevine of staffers, assistants and various support personnel was a particularly well informed one. She'd been part of it herself once, not so very long ago. She pushed open the door to the inner office, then turned in the doorway to issue a few more rapid-fire instructions. "After you've connected me with Mike's office, see what you can do about setting up a meeting with Costner and his agent. I need an answer from them as soon as possible. Then Fed Ex a copy of the script Amy Heckerling's office sent over to my mother in Paris and tell her I think we should find a way to do a deal. Call Jane Jenkins at The Casting Company and find out if she has any more audition tapes ready for me to look at yet. And then . . . let's see—" she pinched the bridge of her nose with two fingers, thinking "—get a fax off to Oliver Stone and tell him that if he can bring the cost down, we'll have a deal. Get a hold of Katzenberg at Disney and ask if we can reschedule Monday's meeting. Call Goldie Hawn's office and tell her absolutely yes, we're interested, but that the soonest we could get together and talk about it would be the middle of next week. Ask her if we could do lunch. And then get me the file on Rafael Santana. I want to go over it one more time before our meeting this afternoon. Got all that?"

"Got it," Robert said, striking the tip of his pencil against his steno pad with a flourish.

Claire nodded and stepped into her office, closing the door behind her. It was blessedly quiet and cool. The soothing colors and the elegant decor calmed and relaxed the senses. The long ivory drapes were closed, shutting out the bright morning sunlight. The soft hum of the air conditioner masked the sounds of moviemaking and commerce outside the building. The gray brocade love seat sitting in front of the delicate Queen Anne table she used as a desk looked wonderfully inviting.

She'd been up since six-thirty, battling the smog and traffic on the L.A. freeways by seven, rushing to make a seven-thirty breakfast meeting at Hugo's. Claire hated rushing, but she'd been unable to slip away from last night's party until the wee hours and she'd overslept, pushing her whole day into overdrive. She also had a tension headache building behind her eyes, the kind that climbed up through the back of her neck and threatened to turn into a real doozy unless she did something, soon, to prevent it from going any further. What she would have liked to do was take a nap until it went away, but the love seat was really too short for anything but sitting. Besides, she didn't have time. The red light on her telephone had blinked on, telling her that Robert was making her call to Mike Ovitz. One didn't keep the powerful chairman of the Creative Arts Agency waiting, not if one wanted to continue eating lunch in Hollywood.

Claire moved behind her desk and sat down. She picked up the telephone receiver and put it to her ear, ready to take over the second Robert made the connection. Twenty minutes later, the rumors she'd heard at Hugo's confirmed and others speculated upon and dissected, Claire broke the connection and buzzed her assistant. "I'm ready for the Santana files now," she said crisply, and cradled the receiver.

"I thought you'd like a nice cup of hot tea first," Robert said as he entered her office in answer to her summons. He placed the delicate white china cup and saucer on the desk in front of her. "And here's a couple of aspirin."

Claire smiled up at him gratefully. "How did you know?"

"You were pinching the bridge of your nose." He dropped the aspirin into her cupped palm. "Rough night?"

"Long. Party at the Spellings. It went until late." She took a sip of the tea. "Ah, that's wonderful. Nobody brews tea like you do, Robert." She took another sip and then set the cup aside, a signal to her assistant that her mind was once again on business.

Robert took the hint. "Your meeting with Mr. Katzenberg has been rescheduled," he reported. "Kevin Costner's agent wasn't available, but I left a message with his secretary. Ms. Hawn said there's no hurry, next week will be fine. Jane Jenkins at The Casting Company said she has three very good possibilities for the role of Molly but she's only got tapes on two of them so far. She'll send those over by messenger this afternoon and get the third one to you by the first of next week." He put a thick manila folder down in front of her. "Here's your mail." A second folder went on top of the first. "The daily production reports." A third folder joined the other two. "And miscellaneous info for you to look over when you have time. You'll like the piece *Premiere* magazine did on *Made For Each Other*," he added. "It's short but sweet."

"Oh?" *Made For Each Other* was her brother Pierce's latest movie, a romantic comedy being shot on location in Toronto. The industry considered it a stretch for Pierce, who was famous for his roles as a macho action-adventure hero. Rumors about the way he was—or wasn't—handling the role had been floating around for weeks now. "What did they say?"

"The writer seems to think the role of Matt Gleason will, and I quote, 'Show a side of the macho superstar the public has never seen before, establishing Pierce Kingston as a viable contender for the crown of the late Cary Grant,' unquote."

"Good ol' Pierce," Claire said fondly, thinking of the way her brother had resisted the part when she'd first suggested it to him. "I knew he could do it." She tilted her head toward the stack of folders on her desk. "Anything else that needs my immediate attention?"

"You might want to look at the *Entertainment Weekly* article on influential women in Hollywood when you get a chance. It came out in this week's issue. Makes your mother sound like a cross between Joan of Arc, Joan Crawford and Audrey Hepburn."

Claire grinned at his description. "Fax it to her, will you, please? She'll get a kick out of it."

"Did that as soon as I got in this morning."

"Good. Then I guess that will do it for now." She picked up the three folders as she spoke and set them aside to look at later. "Let's have the file on Santana," she said, indicating the space she'd made on the gray leather desk blotter in front of her. "Well?" she asked, glancing up when the file failed to appear under her nose. The expression on her assistant's face brought a frown to hers.

"Okay, Robert." She sighed, belatedly noticing the tabloid newspaper on top of the single remaining folder in the crook of his arm. The tension in the back of her neck increased, intensifying the throbbing behind her eyes. She took a fortifying sip of the hot tea. "What is it this time? Has Dad gone off the deep end over some starlet again?" Barry Kingston was a notorious womanizer, an Oscar-winning director whose legendary charm attracted women and publicity in equal measures.

Robert shook his head.

"Another disaster story on Tara and the new baby?" Claire guessed. Tara was the wife of her oldest brother, Gage. An ex-soap-opera vixen who hadn't been in front of a movie camera for over three years, she was still a favorite target of the tabloids. "Or are they predicting the imminent breakup of Pierce and Nikki's marriage again?" They'd been predicting that event ever since her superstar brother had married his bodyguard in a lavish wedding last Valentine's Day.

"None of the above," Robert said. "It's you. You're on the front page of the *National Enquirer.*"

"*Me?*" The word was a squeak of surprise. Claire didn't make the front pages of the tabloids very often these days, not since she'd quit working in front of the camera and started working behind it. "Why?"

"Because of an intimate little dinner you had with Don Johnson, apparently."

"An intimate dinner . . . ?"

"'The Ice Queen Comes Between Hollywood's Hottest Couple,'" Robert said, quoting the headline as he laid the paper on the desk in front of her.

"Hollywood's hottest cou— Oh, my God." She instantly recalled the exact moment the picture had been taken. They'd been coming out of Spago. She'd put her hand on Don's forearm—a brief touch only, to alert him to the presence of the photographer—and he'd turned his head toward her, a query in his easy smile. Claire had to admit that they looked terribly cozy. Intimate, even. As if they were sharing secrets. From the way the picture was cropped, it was impossible to tell that Melanie Griffith—Don Johnson's beautiful, loving and much-loved wife—was on his other side with her hand firmly clasped in his. The three of them had just had dinner together; they'd been discussing the possibility of the two stars appearing in a future Kingston production.

Unconsciously Claire curled her hands into fists, resisting the urge to crumple the paper into a ball and hurl it across the room. God, she hated this kind of sly speculation and innuendo! The outright lies presented as perfect truth. The unctuous smarminess of it. She told herself she should be used to it. Or able to ignore it, at least. But she hated it. Always had and always would.

"Well, it's a good picture, anyway," Robert said into the silence.

Claire felt some of the tension in her neck relax at his words. It sounded like something Pierce would have said. Was, in fact, an echo of the very words her brother had used on other occasions when the media had taken liberties with the truth.

Claire sighed. "They spelled my name right, too."

That was another of Pierce's bromides. Any publicity was good publicity as long as they spelled your name right. The thought helped her. A little. She thought that hitting someone would have helped a lot more, but Claire never resorted to making a public spectacle of herself. Or even a private one.

Very deliberately and calmly, she folded the tabloid in half. "Send a dozen roses to Melanie with a note saying I'm sorry about this," she instructed, and dropped the paper into the wastebasket beneath her desk in a gesture of utter contempt. She glanced at the folder in the crook of her assistant's arm. "Is that the file on Santana?"

Robert nodded. "There isn't anything new since the last time you looked at it," he apologized as he laid it down on the desk in front of his boss. "The man's not what you would call a Hollywood insider. He hasn't been in the business all that long, for one thing. Not as a director, anyway. And he doesn't seem to socialize much. Doesn't attend any of the A-list parties. Or B-list parties, for that matter. No dinners at Spago or anything like that. No flashy starlets on his arm. No big-time charity events. No rumors of hanky-panky on the set. Kind of boring, if you ask me."

Claire nodded absently, as if in agreement, but she wasn't really listening.

Rafael Santana's work is brilliant, she was thinking as she flipped the file open and began to reread the contents. *Really brilliant.* Especially considering the fact that he had no real background in moviemaking.

He'd briefly worked as a stuntman, doubling for Stallone, Seagal and other action-adventure types. And then, out of the blue, apparently, he decided to take up directing.

His documentary on the plight of poverty-stricken Mexican nationals employed at slave wages by greedy giants of American industry had been a masterpiece. It had pulled at the viewers' heartstrings, inciting them to righteous indignation and outrage without descending into the cheap theatrics of propaganda. And it had earned an Oscar nomination for Best Documentary.

The two low-budget action movies he'd done since then were jewels of their kind, appealing to their target audience by staying within the boundaries of the genre while, at the same time, drawing in a wider and more mature segment of the moviegoing public with the subtlety and depth usually expected of mainstream films. In the midst of all the rock-'em, sock-'em, slam-bang action, he'd made the audience really care about the characters, getting more out of the scripts than what had been on paper. She especially liked the way he'd handled the women's roles, imbuing the female leads with a humor and intelligence that made them more than just decorative bimbos.

Creatively, he was exactly what she was looking for.

Moneywise, he was a bargain.

It was his directorial style that worried her.

According to the reports of co-workers, Rafael Santana ran a loose set but he ran it *his* way. Those who weren't comfortable with that saw him as autocratic, stubborn and shockingly lackadaisical regarding the time-honored traditions of moviemaking. Those who liked the way he worked called him innovative, inventive and refreshingly spontaneous in his approach toward the moribund conventions of the industry.

Reports from the producer on his last picture suggested he was inclined to wing it more often than Claire would have liked, eschewing the normal half-a-dozen rehearsals and run-throughs in favor of capturing the freshness of a first take. On the other hand, it also appeared that he wasn't above keeping a crew late into the night—on overtime—shooting and reshooting a scene fifty or sixty times until he got exactly what he wanted from the actors.

He didn't use storyboards except for complicated stunts or scenes with a lot of characters and movement, something else that made Claire nervous since it would make it more difficult to anticipate costs and shooting schedules as closely as she would like.

Worst of all, it appeared he wasn't above modifying the script in the middle of shooting if he thought it would work better. And Claire considered the script of *Desperado* just about perfect the way it was.

It was enough to make a logical, by-the-numbers producer who valued her sanity run screaming just as fast as she could in the opposite direction. And she might have done just that, except . . .

His last producer had had nothing but praise for his inventiveness and the innovative results of what sometimes appeared to be a slapdash method of directing. The actors he'd worked with professed to love him despite his breakneck style, because he got more out of them than they knew was there. The editors she'd talked to had all extolled his film sense, claiming he had that special, unteachable talent the best directors seemed to have for knowing just exactly what scenes were going to be needed to get the story across without wasting a lot of footage in the process.

And then there were the movies themselves; they spoke more eloquently of his talent than any report in the file.

Claire closed the folder with a decisive gesture.

There wasn't a doubt in her mind. Rafael Santana might be a Hollywood outsider, a loose cannon and a virtual unknown, but he was the man she wanted to direct *Desperado*. She had something to prove with this project—to herself, to her family, to Hollywood—and she needed him to help her prove it.

2

THE BUZZER ON Claire's telephone intercom issued two short beeps, the prearranged signal between her and Robert that her four-o'clock appointment had arrived. She glanced at the slender Rolex on her wrist. It was 4:10 p.m. She picked up the receiver. "Tell him I'm on the phone, wait fifteen minutes, then show him in," she instructed her assistant as she slipped her feet into the cream-colored Chanel sling-backs she'd discarded under her desk.

She detested these little power games, but she knew how to play them as well as anyone in the business. Rafael Santana had kept her waiting, whether deliberately or not, so she would keep him waiting just a few minutes longer. It was petty but necessary.

Who waited for whom was a measure of power in Hollywood, just like a choice studio lot parking spot, a corner table at Spago or the biggest, fanciest trailer on location. And it was always best to deal from a position of power, especially if you were a woman. The movie industry wasn't particularly kind to the female of the species; the good ol' boys who ran it would trample all over a lady, given half a chance. Claire had learned early not to give them any chance at all if she could possibly help it.

At 4:12 p.m., she aligned the script of *Desperado* more precisely with the edge of her Queen Anne desk, opened a manila folder on top of her gray leather blotter and laid her enameled Mont Blanc pen at an angle across it, setting the scene to make it look as if she'd been interrupted in the middle of work.

At 4:15 p.m., she adjusted the position of the pen a fraction of an inch.

At 4:18 p.m., she straightened the collarless lapels of her pale blue bouclé Chanel jacket, fingered the single strand of large milky pearls resting against the front of her ivory silk blouse, and smoothed a nonexistent tendril of hair into her flawless chignon.

At 4:22 p.m., she rose to her feet behind her desk and, five seconds later, sat down again, deciding it would make more of a statement if she remained seated until after Santana was ushered into her office.

At 4:24 p.m., she told herself to settle down and quit acting like a rookie assistant producer.

She'd had this same meeting a dozen times before. Two dozen times before. And with seasoned Hollywood insiders ten times more wily and intimidating than one neophyte director could possibly be. She could handle him. She knew the drill. Knew every thrust and parry. Every in and out. She knew the business so well, in fact, that her brothers bragged she could give Donald Trump lessons in the art of the deal, Hollywood style. Just because the deal was more important to her this time didn't mean she should, or would, play it any differently.

"So calm down," she ordered herself as the door to her office opened. She grabbed the pen and bent her head over the open folder on her desk. "One minute," she said without looking up. "I want to get this down before I forget it." She scribbled the first line of her two-year-old nephew's favorite nursery rhyme across the top of the page. "Yes, Robert?" she asked as she lifted her head. Her hand was still poised over the open folder. "What is it?"

"Mr. Santana is here to see you, Ms. Kingston," Robert said, as formal as a well-trained English butler.

Very deliberately, Claire laid her pen down and transferred her gaze to the man standing in the doorway behind and to the left of her executive assistant.

The half-formed smile of professional welcome died on her lips. The fine hairs on the back of her neck rose in automatic, unreasoning response. The muscles in her throat tightened almost painfully.

Rafael Santana was the kind of man she distrusted on sight. One of those flagrantly masculine men, all muscles and machismo, with the dark, brooding sensuality of one of Lucifer's own angels. Tall and powerfully built, he had the shoulders of a defensive lineman and the thighs of a running back. He was dressed to intimidate mere mortals. Deliberately, she was sure. Black cowboy boots with curved heels added another inch to his already impressive height; snug black jeans clung to the muscles in his long legs; a plain black shirt called attention to the hard wall of his broad chest; a black western-cut jacket emphasized the width of his shoulders.

His hair was black, too. Raven black. Ink black. Midnight black. He wore it in a careless style, the soft waves brushed back from the sharp, angular bones of his face. His skin was deep golden brown, shadowed by the late-afternoon stubble that darkened his chiseled jawline and the arrogant thrust of his chin. His eyes were the color of hot espresso coffee.

They were hard eyes, Claire thought. Knowing eyes. Bold, audacious eyes that assessed her as carefully as she assessed him. He stood in the open doorway, his stance casual but alert, as still as a stalking cat with a bird in its sights. Blatant sexuality and raw male power radiated from him like heat from a bonfire.

Claire could feel its uncomfortable warmth all the way across the room and she resolved, then and there, to ignore it. To pretend that it had absolutely no effect on her. She was, after all, a seasoned pro when it came to pretending.

Ruthlessly quelling the impulse to touch her hand to the tingling at the back of her neck, she swallowed to ease the tightness in her throat and smiled graciously. But not *too* graciously. "Please forgive me for keeping you waiting, Mr. Santana," she said, grateful to note that she sounded as cool and calm as she always did. She gestured to the telephone. "I'm afraid it was unavoidable."

He tipped his head slightly, as if in acknowledgment of her apology, but his dark eyes mocked her for the polite social lie that tripped so easily off her tongue.

Claire stood up behind her desk, determined to let him know just exactly who the boss was here. It was always best to begin as you meant to go on. And she meant to be in charge. *Had* to be in charge, especially with a man like this one. There must be no ambiguities. No basis for any misunderstandings that might come back to haunt her later.

"Would you bring me a cup of tea, please, Robert?" she said in her most authoritative voice. "And—" she glanced at the big man still standing, unmoving, in the doorway between the two offices "—coffee?" she guessed, lifting a perfectly arched eyebrow as she waited for his reply.

"Coffee'll do fine."

His voice, Claire thought with a shiver, was as dark and dangerous as the rest of him. It was low pitched and gravelly, like fine whiskey poured through coarse sand. A voice for whispering threats or offering deals that couldn't be refused.

"Sugar, no cream," he added, stepping out of the way as Robert turned to do his boss's bidding.

Claire had to stifle the insane impulse to call her assistant back as he disappeared into his own office. *Don't leave me alone with him!* she wanted to say. But she didn't. She lifted her chin to its haughtiest angle instead, determined to deal with Rafael Santana like the strong, rational woman she knew herself to be. She wasn't an inexperienced little ingenue anymore, for heaven's sake, and he wasn't some kind of a mythological beast who ate ingenues for breakfast. He was a director waiting to find out if she was going to offer him a job. And that put her firmly in the power position here, she reminded herself. *She* was the one who held all the cards—and it was time she made him acknowledge it.

She gave him her frostiest, most intimidating look— the one that had caused the tabloids to christen her the Ice Queen when she was barely twenty-one years old— and motioned toward the brocade love seat in front of her desk. "Why don't you come in and sit down, Mr. Santana?" she said crisply. "We have a great deal to discuss before I can make any decisions."

He didn't move from his spot by the door. "You sure got him well trained," he drawled, the direction of his gaze letting her know he was referring to the way Robert had hustled to carry out her orders.

"Yes," Claire said evenly, deliberately choosing to respond to his words and not the low, sardonic tone. "Robert's an excellent assistant." She motioned toward the love seat again. "Shall we get started, Mr. Santana?"

"Rafe," he said as he began, finally, to amble across the room.

"I beg your pardon?" she murmured stiffly, her whole body tensing as she realized his slow, rolling gait wasn't taking him toward the love seat.

"My name." He stopped two feet in front of her. "It's Rafe," he said, and lifted his hand.

It took every ounce of willpower Claire possessed to keep from shrinking back as he reached out to her, but she held her ground. Every nerve, every fiber of her being was focused on fighting the awful panicky feeling that was fluttering to life beneath her rib cage. He was so overpoweringly male. So dark. So big. So—

"Where I come from, we shake hands before we get down to business," he prompted, looking pointedly at the hand still hanging by her side.

"Oh. Oh, yes. Yes, of course." The panic receded a bit as embarrassment took its place. "How stupid of me. I don't know where my mind was . . ." she murmured. "That telephone call, I guess . . ."

She offered her hand reluctantly, watching it disappear in his as he closed his fingers around it, feeling the heat of his big, hard palm against hers. It shocked her, that heat, warming her skin and the blood that flowed beneath it. She wanted desperately to pull away before she got burned.

"It's a pleasure to meet you, Mr. Santana." She pumped his hand once, briskly, for form's sake, and started to withdraw.

His fingers tightened on hers, holding her hand where it was.

She looked up at him, her wide blue eyes made wider by uncertainty, the uneasy feeling in her stomach returning, increasing exponentially for every fraction of a second he continued to hold her hand. She sucked in her breath, ready to forget pride and her precious control and yell for Robert to come and save her. From what, she didn't know.

"The pleasure's mine," he said, staring down at her. "And, like I said, the name's Rafe." And then he smiled. A slow, lazy smile that softened the harsh lines of his face. "Actually—" his gravelly voice softened, too, becoming dangerously seductive "—it's Rafael. Rafael Enrique Santana. But only my mama calls me that." The smile widened a fraction, deepening the little wrinkles etched in the skin around his dark eyes. "And then only when she's mad enough to holler at me."

And then, just like that, he let go of her hand and turned away, sauntering around the desk to the love seat.

Claire let out her breath and began to breathe normally again, oddly relieved to know he had a mother. He wasn't some big, dark, overpowering beast intent on doing her bodily harm; he was a human being with a mother who hollered at him. And he smiled when he thought of her. How dangerous could he be?

RAFE FOLDED HIMSELF into the uncomfortable little love seat, lifting one booted ankle to rest it on his opposite knee, and tapped the rolled-up copy of *Desperado* in his left hand against his thigh as he waited for Claire Kingston's next move. She stood behind her fancy excuse for a desk, a wary, considering look in her wide blue eyes, staring down her nose at him as if he were some kind of wild animal who'd been set loose in her office. Or some ravening beast who would jump her the first chance he got.

As if he'd waste his time trying to get close to an icicle like her, he thought, scowling ferociously at the toe of his boot. But even as he thought it, he knew he lied.

Just the way the photographs had lied.

Oh, they'd captured her icy elegance well enough and that high-toned aristocratic snootiness that made him long to take her down a peg or two. But they'd completely missed the sensuality simmering beneath her frosty surface. The Ice Queen might be cold but she wasn't frozen. Not by a long shot.

True, the body under that prissy little suit was as reed slender as it appeared in photographs, but the graceful, feminine way she moved it was an unthinking invitation to anyone with enough testosterone in his blood to recognize it and respond accordingly. Her skin really was as pale and flawless as the fine porcelain it resembled, but it had a warm, translucent, touchable quality not discernible from a mere photograph. And her perfect cupid's bow of a mouth was even more lush than it had seemed to be.

But it was her eyes that gave her true nature away. Beneath the icy calm of her expression was a bubbling cauldron of emotions no camera could hope to capture.

He'd seen it clearly when she looked up at him. Felt it in the way her slender hand trembled ever so slightly in his. Heard it in the quick little intake of her breath. Sensed it in the way she'd tensed up and started to withdraw—and then didn't. She'd been affected by him, all right, and determined to hide it. The pampered princess was shocked by her gut-level response to a mere peasant. It made him mad, a little, but it also made him wonder. What would it take to make the Ice Queen melt, and just how hot would she burn when she did?

Not that he had any real intention of finding out. At least, he amended, not until they'd gotten a few other things ironed out first. Like his contract for *Desperado*. No woman, no matter how intriguing a challenge she presented, was worth more to him right now than a chance to direct the next Kingston production. Not even a tempting little princess like Claire Kingston.

"Is that acceptable to you, Mr. Santana?" she asked sharply, intruding on his mind's fevered wanderings.

She had a voice like vanilla ice cream, he thought idly, deliberately making her wait a little longer for his attention. It was delectably rich and smooth. Delicately sweet. And cold enough to give a man a bad case of brain frost if he wasn't careful.

"Mr. Santana?"

He lifted his gaze from his contemplation of the squared-off toe of his boot—slowly, moving only his eyes—and found her sitting behind her desk, staring at him. Her perfect cherry-red lips were pressed together like an impatient and disapproving schoolteacher's as she waited for his answer. They looked utterly delicious.

"Is what acceptable, Ms. Kingston?" he asked.

"The general terms of the contract I sent to you. I assume you've had a chance to at least look it over."

Rafe shook his head. "General terms are never acceptable." He shifted his upraised foot to the floor and leaned forward, elbows on his splayed knees, the script in one hand, ready to settle into some serious dealing. "Let's get down to specifics, shall we?"

Claire recognized the posture of someone ready to deal. She folded her hands together on top of her desk and fastened her eyes on his, pretending to herself that she didn't notice the way his hair fell over his forehead as he leaned forward. Or the careless, utterly masculine way he raked it back with the fingers of one big hand. "Which specifics are you interested in, Mr. Santana?" she asked.

"Casting."

"We're still working on it. I've seen a few audition tapes, and The Casting Company will be sending over more later this week, but I haven't had anyone in for a reading yet."

He digested that information for a moment. Audition tapes and readings meant she wasn't planning on any big stars to carry the picture. Well, that was okay, he decided. Done right, *Desperado* was the kind of screenplay that could succeed with or without a name in the title role. And he intended to do it right.

"All right," he agreed. "But I'll want approval on the final choices."

Claire lifted an elegant eyebrow. "I admire your . . .

ambition," she said, letting him know just what she
thought of his request, "but I'm afraid that's out of the
question."

Rafe looked her right in the eyes, knowing that this
was where he would take his stand and test her mettle.
And, maybe, lose his big chance to direct a Kingston
production. He tried not to think about that.

"Then I'm afraid this discussion is over." He spoke
the words with steely calm. "That particular specific is
nonnegotiable."

Claire could tell from his body posture and the look
in his eyes that he meant it. He'd walk if she said no. She
nodded. "Cast approval," she agreed.

Rafe stifled a sigh of relief. "All right, then." He
knew, now, just how much she wanted him for this
project. And just how much bargaining power he had.
"Budget?"

"Twelve million," she said firmly. "Absolute tops."

He let disbelief show plainly on his face. "For a
Kingston production?"

"You've read the script. *Desperado* is a small movie.
A character study," she said. "No special effects. No
fancy stunts. No big names. Twelve million is plenty."

"How much of that is mine?" he asked, because he
knew she expected him to. He didn't really care if any
of it was his. Hell, he'd pay her to let him direct the
movie. But it wouldn't do to let her know that.

"Four hundred thousand."

Rafe frowned, trying to look as if four hundred
thousand dollars was mere chicken feed when, in truth,

it meant he would be able to fully finance the college educations of his two youngest brothers. And pay for renovations to the old family homestead his mother refused to move out of. And still be able to put something aside for a rainy day.

Robert came back into the room, then, intruding into the silence, and set a heavily laden silver tray down on the edge of Claire's desk. It held two small china pots, two delicate china cups with matching saucers and a small plate of frosted tea cakes and fancy shortbread cookies.

Claire absently smiled her thanks at him, her attention never really leaving the man sitting across from her. Rafe didn't even look up from his contemplation of the script he held in his hand. Robert poured out their beverages and exited the office as silently as he had entered it.

"There's a bonus if you bring it in under schedule," Claire said craftily, trying to sweeten the deal.

Rafe shrugged and tossed the script down onto the love seat next to him. "How much of a bonus?" he asked, and reached for his coffee cup.

"That depends on how much under schedule it is," Claire said, watching him try to stick his finger through the delicate handle. It wouldn't fit. He curved his long fingers around the cup, instead.

"And the projected schedule is what?" he asked, looking at her over the silver-edged rim.

Claire quickly redirected her gaze to meet his. "Not projected," she said. "Already set in stone. The continuity breakdown and shooting schedule have already been done." She knew because she'd done them. "Forty-eight days."

Rafe pretended to consider that as he took another long sip of his coffee. Forty-eight days was more than enough time. Particularly since he'd already roughed out a forty-day shooting schedule in his own mind. "Okay, forty-eight days." He nodded slowly, as if it hurt him to agree to her stringent requirements. He indicated the script. "When do I meet the writer?"

Claire clasped her hands just a bit tighter. "You don't."

Rafe didn't need to feign his look of disbelief. "I don't?"

Claire nodded. "That's right. You don't."

Rafe reached out and set his coffee cup back on its white china saucer. "Why the hell not?"

Claire lifted an imperious eyebrow. "Is there any particular reason you need to?"

"Scenes twenty-four through thirty-one need work. They drag."

Claire concealed her spurt of annoyance at his blunt assessment. "I'll convey your concerns," she said, neglecting to mention that she, too, had been bothered by those particular scenes. "And get back to you on it before shooting begins."

"And that's it?"

Claire nodded. "That's it."

"No discussion? No hashing it out? No story conference? Just you'll convey my concerns to the writer and get back to me?"

"Yes."

"Who the hell is—" he reached over and smoothed the script flat "—K.E.C.?" he said, reading the byline out loud.

"K.E.C. is a very private person," Claire said, giving him the details she'd decided on earlier. "A recluse, if you will, who attached certain conditions to the sale of that script. One of them was absolute anonymity. The other was absolutely no script changes except by the original writer. Kingston Productions was more than happy to meet those conditions." She leveled a look at Rafe over the desk. There was steel in her wide blue eyes as they met his. And a knot as big as an orange in her stomach. "If you don't feel you can go along with that, then we can consider this discussion at an end now."

Rafe didn't have to think about it. He didn't even pretend to. "Is the rest of the creative staff going to insist on anonymity, too?" he asked, the sarcastic edge in his voice letting her know he wasn't happy with the situation even though he was agreeing to it.

Claire ruthlessly suppressed the spurt of elation she felt at his capitulation. She hadn't won completely. Not yet. "No, of course not," she said calmly. "I'll have Robert schedule a meeting with the rest of the creative staff just as soon as we can agree on who they are."

"I'll want the same assistant director I used on my last two pictures," Rafe warned, not wanting to give in too easily.

"Fine," Claire said. The assistant director he'd used on his last two pictures was his sister, which could conceivably cause problems since one of the AD's jobs was to play watchdog for the producer. But Claire discounted that. She planned to be on the set to play watchdog herself, all day, every day.

"And Becky Ward for art direction."

Claire pretended to consider that. "Fine," she agreed after a moment, not telling him that Becky was her first choice for art director, too.

"And Dennis Cleary for cinematography," he challenged, fully expecting her to refuse.

Claire knew exactly what he expected. She smiled. "Fine."

He gave her a long, considering look. "You're not going to insist on your brother?"

"Gage is the best there is, but he's way too expensive for this project." And she didn't want any member of her talented and illustrious family anywhere near *Desperado*. It would sink or swim on the talents of one Kingston alone. "Besides, he's busy on something else. If Dennis Cleary is available and within the budget, you can have him. Anything else?"

Rafe hesitated and then, *Oh, what the hell*, he thought. It was worth a try. "Approval of the final cut."

"I wouldn't give Eastwood final approval," she said dryly. "And he's got an Oscar." She lifted that elegant eyebrow at him again. "What've you got? Other than a vastly overinflated opinion of your worth?" she added hastily as she saw his lips begin to curve upward.

"Well, now." He relaxed back against the love seat—all six feet four inches of latent masculine power—and flashed her a lazy, arrogant grin. "I guess you'll just have to find that out for yourself, won't you?"

Only sheer stubbornness and the certain knowledge that he'd take full advantage of any sign of weakness kept Claire from backing down from the challenge inherent in that renegade grin. She flicked a contemptuous glance down his long, hard body, just to prove it held no allure for her. And no threat, either.

"Yes," she said, and her voice dripped ice water. "I guess I will." She stood, pushing her chair back with her legs as she rose. "So. Do we have a deal, Mr. Santana?"

He rose, too, and took a step forward. "The name's Rafe and, yes—" he extended his right hand over the desk "—we have a deal."

"Rafe," she said, and put her hand in his to seal the bargain.

3

"*You're* the production manager?"

Claire looked up from the cross-plot board she was reviewing one last time before the first preproduction meeting of *Desperado* began. Her director was glaring at her from behind her desk. He held the shooting schedule she'd given him to look over, the one with her name in two places on every page.

"Yes, I'm the production manager," she said, as cool as if butter wouldn't melt in her mouth. Her blue eyes widened innocently. "Didn't I mention that the other day?"

"You did not."

"Oh." She shrugged. "Well, I'm mentioning it now." She turned her back on him to straighten a vertical scene-strip on the cross-plot board as if its correct placement was the only thing on her mind. "I hope it's not going to be a problem for you," she said, knowing it was, because it would be for just about any director worth his salt.

"Hell, yes, it's going to be a problem for me. I should think it would be a problem for you, too."

"Really?" She tossed the word over her shoulder. "In what way?"

"Don't play innocent with me, Claire. You know damn well in what way. A producer's job is to take care of the big picture and let his—excuse me, *her*—production staff handle the day-to-day stuff. It screws up the chain of command if the producer is always on the set, sticking her nose into every little thing that comes up. Undermining everyone else's authority."

"I won't be on the set as the producer. I'll be on the set as the production manager. And I don't plan to stick my nose into anything," she assured him airily, still studying the arrangement of the scene-strips. "So that should settle it nicely, shouldn't it?"

"No, that does not settle it. Nicely or otherwise." Rafe tossed the shooting schedules down onto the desk and moved around it to confront her more directly. "I don't work well with someone hanging over my shoulder every minute, trying to second-guess me and countermanding my orders." He reached out and grasped her chin, turning her head around so he could argue face-to-face. "No set can operate with two bosses," he informed her with a growl. "Especially not mine."

Claire told herself there was no reason to panic. Nothing could happen with Robert in the next room and the rest of the production staff due to arrive any minute. She reached up and, slowly, carefully, pushed Rafe's hand away, giving him a look that could flash-freeze lava while she did it.

"I have no intention of hanging over your shoulder or usurping your authority. Or anyone else's, for that matter," she said, managing to sound composed and in control despite the unruly way her heart had begun to beat. "On the set, you're in charge, you run things your way and I'm just the production manager."

She stepped back and turned, pacing, unconsciously putting the length of the four-foot cross-plot board between them before she turned to face him again.

"You have my promise that any concerns I have as a producer will be handled away from the set, after shooting is through for the day," she assured him, calmer now that there was a few feet of space between them.

"And just how do you intend to manage that little balancing act?"

She gave him an arch look. "I imagine the same way the assistant director was planning to balance being the producer's watchdog and your sister, too."

"Is that what this is about? You don't think Pilar will look after your interests on the set, so you've decided to look after them yourself?"

"I don't even know Pilar yet," Claire said reasonably. "And I appointed myself production manager on this movie long before I knew she was going to be your AD. Or, for that matter, before I decided to offer you the job as director." She reached out and adjusted another scene-strip with careful precision. "It's a business decision that has nothing to do with either of you."

"Does your mother know about this business decision?"

"My mother?" she asked, without looking at him. "What does my mother have to do with this?"

"She's the brains behind this outfit, isn't she? The executive producer on all Kingston Productions? You can't tell me one of 'Hollywood's Ten Most Influential Women—'" he was referencing the previous week's *Entertainment Weekly* article "—approved this cockamamy scheme of yours."

Claire's head snapped up. "I'm the executive producer of *Desperado*." She rapped out the words like a drill sergeant. "No one else. And, cockamamy scheme or not, what I say goes. If you have a problem with that, Mr. Santana, then let's settle it right now, before the rest of the production staff arrives. Well?" she demanded when he didn't respond. "Shall I find someone else to direct my movie?"

Rafe shook his head in amazement, bemused by the lightning swift change in her. She'd been cool and disdainful a moment before, pushing his hand away as if she were afraid it would leave dirt on her alabaster chin, dismissing his legitimate concerns as if they were nothing more than a nuisance. And then, suddenly, she was as furious as a spitting cat. She stood there with her small, elegant hands fisted on her hips and her chin raised as if daring him to take a poke at it. Her wide blue eyes were full of emotions that were anything but glacial.

"Am I going to need to look for another director or not?" she demanded, haughty as an outraged queen.

Rafe couldn't help it. He grinned. "Not," he said, and was rewarded by the perplexed look that suddenly filled her eyes.

"Well . . . okay, then," she mumbled, taken aback by his abrupt and cheerful about-face. She felt a little silly, too, standing there with her hands on her hips like some scolding fishwife when there was no one to scold. She dropped her hands to her sides and tugged on the hip-length hem of her fitted French blue St. Laurent jacket, struggling to regain her composure. "I guess that's settled then," she said crisply, trying to pretend her embarrassing lapse of control had never occurred.

Rafe's grin widened a teasing, taunting fraction. "Not by a long shot, honey." His long-legged gait covered the scant few feet between them without her quite being aware of it. "You're not getting away with trying to slip something like that by me quite so easily."

"Not getting away with trying to slip . . . ?" Claire tilted her head back, keeping her eyes on his as he approached. "What do you mean, I'm not getting away with trying to slip it by you? I haven't tried to slip any—" Her voice died in her throat as he reached out and touched his fingertip to her lips. She froze.

"That's better." His gravelly voice was rich with satisfaction at having silenced her so effortlessly. "Much better. Now—"

His train of thought abruptly derailed. He'd intended to tell her . . . something. Or make some point about . . . something. But the way she stood there, utterly still, staring up at him with those impossibly blue eyes of hers, drove it right out of his mind.

He brushed his fingertip back and forth slowly over her lips, fascinated by the feel of her. "You've got the sexiest mouth I've ever seen," he murmured huskily. "So soft." He traced the delicate bow of her upper lip. "So sweet." And the lush swell of her lower one. "As tempting and juicy as ripe summer cherries straight off the tree." His finger drifted to her chin on the last few words, and he lifted it, tilting her head back even further. "I'll bet they taste as juicy as they look," he growled, low, and bent his head.

Alarm bells went off inside Claire's head, shrieking at her to move or scream, to slap his hand and back away. But she couldn't move. Couldn't function. All she could do was stand there, frozen like a deer in the headlights of an oncoming car, and wait for her fate.

His head seemed to come toward her in slow motion, every detail as sharp and clear as if she were seeing it through a 250-mm lens. His dark hair fell forward a slow, sensuous degree at a time, brushing against his bronzed forehead as he leaned toward her. His dark eyes loomed hot and fierce, focused intently on his goal. His mouth opened slightly as it descended inexorably toward hers, the lips full and firm and clean edged, parting softly over his strong white teeth, coming closer . . . and closer . . .

There was a sharp rap on the door, loud as a cannon shot in the quiet office. Claire gasped and jumped back.

Rafe swore and dropped his hand. They both had to struggle to control their breathing.

"Excuse me," Robert said as he poked his head around the door. "Mr. Cleary and Ms. Santana are here for the production meeting. Ms. Ward called from her car phone to say she and Mr. Bennington are stuck in traffic and will be here as soon as they can. I haven't heard from any of the others yet. Should I wait until everyone arrives, or send them in as they get here?"

Rafe and Claire glanced at each other, quickly, guiltily, and looked away. "Send them in," they said at the same time.

"WHY NOT WOODY HARRELSON?" Rafe said two days later as they sat at the conference table in Claire's office trying to agree on an actor to play the male lead in *Desperado*. "He's young. He's good-looking. He can project that aw-shucks, hayseed quality we need for Josh. *White Men Can't Jump* showed he's got pull at the box office. And *Indecent Proposal* proved he's got range."

"It also put him way out of the ballpark for this project. We can't afford him."

"Can't you trim the budget someplace else? Cut the schedule," he suggested, gesturing toward the cross-plot board on the easel behind her. It was approximately four feet wide and thirty inches tall, filled with movable quarter-inch strips representing every scene in the movie. It was a major tool for determining the shooting schedule and, thus, the budget. "We're not going to need anywhere near that many days to get this thing in the can."

"I could cut the schedule in half and we still couldn't afford Harrelson."

"Well, I'm sure you can find the money someplace. A really good producer always knows where she can come up with more money." He paused a calculated beat. "You are a good producer, aren't you?"

Claire ignored his little gibe. "We can't afford him," she repeated and waved a hand at the pile of audition tapes on the table between them. "Didn't you like any of those guys?"

Rafe shook his head. "Neither did you."

"What makes you think that?"

"Not think. Know." He gave her a slow, lazy smile, just like the one he'd given her the first time they met. The one that had almost made her believe he couldn't possibly be as dangerous as he looked.

She knew better than to be fooled by that smile now. He was ten times more dangerous than he looked. "And just how do you know?"

"Because if you were the least bit interested in any of them, you'd already have arranged to have him in for a reading, that's how." He cocked an eyebrow at her. "Right?"

"Ah . . . yes, right," Claire said, surprised by his perception, and just a little dismayed by it, too. She didn't know whether to be pleased that he seemed to be adjusting to her working style so quickly. Or appalled that he knew her so well after only a few days.

"WE'VE BEEN LOOKING at these tapes so long, I'm beginning to see double." Rafe leaned back in his chair, rubbing the heels of his hands against his eye sockets as he spoke. "And not one of the actresses we've seen is right for Molly."

"I think you're wrong," Claire countered. She got up from her seat at the conference table and crossed to the country French armoire that housed her television and video recorder. "Look at Christine Bishop again," she said as she slipped another tape into the machine. She pushed the play button and came back to perch on the edge of the table to watch. "I think she'd be perfect."

"She's too sophisticated. Molly's a small-town girl from nowheresville. That woman—" he gestured at the glossy image on the television screen "—isn't small-town anything. She looks...I don't know...too knowing, I guess, to play the trusting, injured innocent."

Claire shook her head. "Molly's injured but she isn't innocent. She's vulnerable. There's a difference. And she isn't all that trusting, either. Josh—" who they *still* hadn't cast "—has to work really hard for her trust. Molly's a lot more knowing than you think." She slanted a look at Rafe out of the corner of her eye. He looked a little ragged around the edges but appealingly rugged; he had the kind of beard that always started to sprout five-o'clock shadow around three in the afternoon. "Most women are."

"Most women are what?" he asked absently, his eyes on the television screen, trying to see whatever it was that Claire saw.

"Less innocent and more knowing than most men think."

The cryptic bite in her voice brought his head around. "Did I miss something here?"

Claire shook her head, already regretting the remark. "Just pointing out a few little known facts of life," she quipped with what she hoped was convincing insouciance. She pointed at the screen with the remote control, trying to redirect his attention. "Watch the way Christine uses her eyes in this scene. See how she looks at him? See the vulnerability? And the determination not to give in to it? Here—" She jabbed rewind with her thumb and backed the tape up a bit, then restarted it and hit mute. "Watch it again without the sound. See?" She leaned forward, gesturing at the flickering image on the television. "Tone down the makeup and the hair, change the clothes, give her a Texas accent and she's perfect. I think we should ask her to come in for a reading." She glanced over at him to gauge his reaction.

He was staring at her as if he'd just had a revelation. "I think you should read for Molly."

"Me?" Her face registered pure, unfeigned astonishment. "I'm not an actress."

"But you were. And a hell of a good one, too. The character you played in *The Deceivers* was a small-town girl like Molly. You're a little too old for the part, of course, but the right makeup and wardrobe would take care of that. You've got the kind of innocence and purity that—"

"No," Claire said vehemently, shaking her head. "I haven't done any acting—or even wanted to—" she'd never really *wanted* to, not even when she was Hollywood's favorite child star "—for seven years."

"That doesn't mean you couldn't go back to it." He leaned forward eagerly, suddenly excited at the idea of directing her, of guiding her, of coaxing her to reveal all those emotions she kept hidden under that brittle coating of ice. The relationship between a director and an actress could be an intensely intimate one, and he wanted, very much, to be intensely intimate with her. "The part of Molly reads like it was written for you. The vulnerability. The determination not to show it." He reached for her hand. "I don't know why I didn't see it before."

Claire hopped off the table before he could touch her. "Don't be ridiculous," she snapped, irritated and absurdly frightened at the same time. What if he realized how close to the truth he'd just come?

"Why is it ridiculous? You were an acclaimed actress. You won an Oscar for your role in *Age Of Consent*," he pointed out, as if she might not remember.

"I was an acclaimed *child* actress." She strode over to the video machine and punched hi-speed rewind, then stood with her back to him, watching the tape as it whirred around. "I won that Oscar when I was thirteen years old."

"So? Lots of child actresses make a successful transition to adult roles. Elizabeth Taylor did it. Natalie Wood. Jodie Foster. You were on your way to doing it yourself with *The Deceivers*. And then you quit."

He remembered the stories that had been printed when she'd disappeared from sight after *The Deceivers* was finished. They'd said she was suffering from anorexia and had been checked into a hospital by her worried family; that she'd had a nervous breakdown; that she'd run off with a married man; developed a disfiguring disease; decided to go to college; joined a bizarre religious cult; been abducted by aliens; given birth to a handicapped baby and selflessly retired from acting to care for it. None of that had been true, of course, and the movie community had finally decided she'd been motivated by nothing more than whatever it was that motivated young actresses to do the crazy things they did.

But looking at her now, staring at the rigidness of her narrow back beneath the pale blue-gray fabric of her suit jacket, Rafe wondered if there hadn't been something to at least one of those stories. Something that might account for the layer of ice she kept wrapped around her emotions.

"Why?" he asked softly. "What makes a successful actress—a young woman who practically grew up in front of the camera—just chuck it all and walk away?"

Claire sighed and stopped the video machine, popping the tape out into her hand. Then, taking a quick breath, she lifted her chin and turned around, prepared to give him the same speech she'd given her family.

"You just captured the 'why' of it yourself," she told him. "I grew up in front of the camera. Literally. My mother was pregnant with me when she did *Trial By Fire* with Sean Connery. When I was four years old, my father cast me in a small bit part in one of his movies. And I just . . . took, I guess. Everyone said I was a natural actress, that I was born to be in front of the camera, but to me, well—" she shrugged "—acting was just something I did, like breathing. When I was a little girl it never occurred to me to wonder whether I enjoyed it or not."

Which she hadn't. Growing up in the constant glare of klieg lights and publicity had its drawbacks, few of which a naturally reticent child could—or later, would—articulate. Her acting career pleased her parents. It provided a framework for her life. It gave her a chance to experience emotions. That was all she needed to know back then.

"I didn't get around to thinking about whether acting was really what I wanted to do with the rest of my life until I was almost nineteen and did *The Deceivers*. When I did finally start to think about it, I decided I didn't want to do it anymore."

"That still doesn't say anything about why."

She gave him a pained look, one that said he should be able to figure it out for himself. "Acting bored me," she said, as if that fact should be self-evident. "It's as simple as that. There wasn't any challenge in it anymore so I decided to try something else. And this—" she spread her hands, indicating the pile of audition tapes on the conference table, the cross-plot board propped up on its easel, the double stacks of unread scripts and treatments piled neatly on her desk "—is that something."

Rafe still wasn't convinced. "And you've never felt the yen to go back to it? The lure of the bright lights. The lust for fame and stardom?"

"No. Never." The words rang with absolute, utter conviction. "So I guess you'd better take another look at this." She slid Christine Bishop's audition tape across the smooth surface of the conference table. "We still need to find an actress to play Molly."

"OKAY, SO YOU WERE RIGHT," Rafe said, giving Claire a sour look across the width of the conference table. He'd been finding out she was right about a lot of things. Claire Kingston was one hell of a producer, he'd discovered, with uncanny instincts about who or what would work in a given movie. "Christine Bishop's reading was—"

"Brilliant," Claire supplied smugly. "Stupendous. Awe inspiring."

"I was going to say adequate," he countered, just to see if he could rile her. It had become a game with him, seeing if he could get the Ice Queen to lose her temper again the way she had when he'd accused her of hatching a cockamamy scheme without her mother's permission. So far, he hadn't had any luck. And it was driving him slowly crazy.

"You're just miffed because you were wrong," Claire said calmly, refusing to allow him to ruffle her. She hadn't lost her temper once since that first time and she intended to keep it that way. It was safer. "Christine's reading was great and you know it. Now all we have to do is find a male lead with the same strength and style."

"I'VE FOUND JOSH," Rafe announced. "And in a place where I wasn't even looking for him. I was clicking through the channels last night and there he was, on a rerun of 'L.A. Law.'"

Claire didn't even look up from the folder full of production reports she was reviewing. "Who and how much?"

"A good journeyman actor," Rafe said, drawing out the details because he knew how much she liked to get right to the point. "Nothing flashy but real solid. He's a little older than the part calls for but—"

Claire lifted her head. "Who and how much?"

"He's an old friend of yours, too. From *The Deceivers*."

"Who and how—" A startled look came into her eyes. "From *The Deceivers*?"

Rafe nodded. "Dax Wyatt," he announced, expecting her to be bowled over by his choice.

"Dax Wyatt?" She stared at him as if he'd lost his mind. "You've got to be kidding."

Rafe frowned. "What's wrong with Dax Wyatt?"

"Well . . ." Claire searched around in her mind for something she could tell him, some excuse she could offer. Anything but the truth. "He's too old, for one thing." She fiddled with the production reports on her desk, briskly stacking them into a more orderly pile. "You said so yourself."

"I also said it wasn't a problem. He's not that much older than what we're looking for. And he can play younger. He's got that down-home, hayseed quality that's so important. And, physically, he'd be a good contrast for Christine. I think we should ask him to come in for a reading."

"No."

"Why not?"

"Because I don't want him, that's why not." Claire closed the file folder with a snap and stood up. "And that's the end of it."

"No, that's not the end of it. Not by a long shot," Rafe said, beginning to get angry. "You can't just make a decision like that by yourself, without at least discussing it with me first. I have cast approval, remember?"

"So do I," she shot back. "And I don't approve of Dax Wyatt."

"Why?"

"Because . . . because I don't like him, that's why." She turned to the credenza behind her desk and opened a file drawer. "So can we just drop it, please?"

"No," he said stubbornly. "No, I don't think we can. Not unless you can give me a good reason why we should. Dax Wyatt is a good actor. I think he'd make a great Josh. And I won't dismiss him from consideration just because you don't like him. Hell, Claire," he said reasonably, "it's not like I'm asking you to go to bed with the guy. I'm just suggesting we give him a reading and—"

The file drawer closed with a loud bang.

Rafe's hot coffee eyes narrowed with sudden speculation. "Is that it? Is that what this is about?" His gaze bored into her back. "You had an affair with Dax Wyatt that ended badly? And now you don't want to work with him because of it?"

"An affair?" Claire's fingers tightened on the curved handle of the file drawer. "You think I had an affair with Dax Wyatt?" For one short, horrifying moment she thought she was going to faint. Or throw up. Or both. And then she mastered herself, through sheer strength of will, and turned around to face him with her Ice Queen persona firmly in place.

"Don't be insulting," she said mildly, as if the whole subject of Dax Wyatt had suddenly started to bore her. "The man is a toad." Her perfect bow of an upper lip lifted in a delicate sneer. "A slimy, chauvinistic toad. And the simple fact is, I prefer not to work with toads if I can possibly help it. But if you think he'd make a good Josh . . ." She shrugged, as if there were no accounting for taste, and reached for the weekly appointment calendar on her desk. "It looks like I have some time later in the week," she said as she ruffled through the pages. "Which day is best for your schedule?" She looked up when he didn't say anything. "Rafe?"

"That was a hell of an about-face."

She didn't pretend to misunderstand. "I owe you one," she said. "After all, you went with my instincts on Christine. It's only fair that I extend the same courtesy to you. Who knows? I might be pleasantly surprised. Dax may have matured since the last time we worked together. Now—" she picked up her Mont Blanc pen "—how does Thursday morning at ten sound to you?"

"YOU'VE GOT TO MAKE a decision, Molly," Dax Wyatt said, reciting the lines from the script. "Either you trust me or you don't." He looked into Christine Bishop's upturned face. "What's it gonna be? You comin' with me or not?" he asked, somehow injecting both who-gives-a-damn carelessness and soul-deep desperation into his voice.

Anyone sitting in a darkened theater would feel his anguish and know, just from his inflection and the look in his eyes, that his heart would break if she didn't decide in his favor. And that he would die before he'd let her know it.

Rafe glanced over at Claire with an I-told-you-so look in his eyes. *Didn't I tell you Dax Wyatt would be perfect for the part?* his look said.

Claire had to agree.

Dax Wyatt was the perfect bad boy in love. Vulnerable but struggling not to show it. Hiding his feelings behind a tough-guy facade. Scared to death of being rejected.

Maybe he *had* matured since the last time she'd worked with him, Claire thought.

"I . . . I can't," Christine Bishop said. "Not now. Not yet. Please—" She put her hand on Dax's arm as he started to turn away. "Josh, please. Just give me a little more time."

"How much time?" he said roughly, and everyone in the room could hear the tears in his voice, although nothing but disdain for her waffling showed in his face.

"Just a few days. Until Mama is better. I'll go with you then. I promise."

"You promised before."

"I mean it this time, Josh. I do. You've got to believe me." She clutched at his shirtfront. "You've got to promise not to leave without me. Please, Josh."

His hands went to her biceps, holding her off. "I can't hang around here forever," he said roughly.

"Just a few more days."

Claire watched his face soften as he looked down at Christine.

"A few more days," he agreed, and pulled her into his arms. Their lips met in a searing kiss, one that went on longer than what the script called for.

Well, he hasn't matured all that much, Claire thought, watching uneasily as Christine wriggled backward, trying to extricate herself from Dax's embrace without being obvious about it.

"I think that will do it," Claire said loudly, unable to watch any longer.

Dax lifted his head with a grin. "How'd I do?" he asked, seemingly unaware that Christine had found his prolonged embrace distasteful.

Rafe looked at Claire. Reluctantly Claire nodded.

"Congratulations," Rafe said. "You've got the part."

"WE'RE ALL AGREED so far, then?" Claire looked around the conference table, sweeping everyone up in her gaze as she made the statement. She and most of her creative and production staff—the art director and set decorator, the assistant director, the script supervisor, the cinematographer and, of course, the director—were at the ragged end of a long and grueling preproduction meeting in what had been a series of long and grueling preproduction meetings. "Everyone understands what we're trying to achieve here, right? We know what we have to do to accomplish it and what our parameters are. And we all know *exactly* what our departmental budgets are, right?"

There were tired nods of agreement and subdued murmurs of assent all around.

"Becky? R.J.?" she said, calling on the creative talents in charge of art direction and set decoration when no one offered further comment. "You're clear about your end of it?"

"Yes, Claire." R. J. Bennington answered for both of them. "Crystal clear."

Claire shifted her gaze to the script supervisor. "Anna? Questions? Comments?"

Anna Markowitz took off her glasses and rubbed the bridge of her nose. "If I think of anything we haven't already covered a million times, I'll let you know."

"Pilar? Anything you think we've forgotten?"

"Not a thing, Claire. You've pretty much covered it all."

"Over and over and over again," Rafe muttered, sotto voce.

Everyone laughed, even Claire. But then she got right back down to business. "Dennis? How about you? Do you have any concerns we haven't nailed down yet?"

The cinematographer didn't even open his eyes. "Location."

No one had to ask what he meant.

After three weeks of looking for the right small town to represent the fictional Burley, Texas, the location manager still hadn't come up with anything to suit Claire's stringent standards. And time was running short. They were supposed to start shooting in less than two weeks.

"I've got that covered. Or should I say, we've got that covered," she amended, casting a quick glance at her director. "Rafe and I are leaving for Texas bright and early Sunday morning," she informed them, trying to sound as if the very thought didn't have her shaking in her Chanel pumps.

Driving a rental car through small West Texas towns, eating at rural cafés that featured chicken-fried everything and sleeping in tiny motels with no room service or cable TV wasn't something she was looking forward to. Especially not with Rafe Santana sitting in that rental car beside her, sharing those meals and sleeping in the room next to hers.

"I promise we'll find Burley in plenty of time for all of you to get out there and look it over before we start shooting," she assured them, silently promising herself that it would be the shortest location hunt on record, "even if I have to build it with my bare hands."

"Hear, hear," Becky Ward said. And then yawned. "Can we go home now?"

Claire sighed like the long-suffering and put-upon mother of six. "Yes, you can all go home now. We're finished for today. Robert will let you all know the minute we've settled on a location," she said as they began pushing away from the conference table. "And everyone knows about keeping everyone else abreast of all their plans through Robert, as well, right?" she added, unable to resist a last reminder. "Any last minute changes should be in writing or—"

Rafe reached around her and put his hand firmly over her mouth, cutting off the flow of words. "We *know*," he said. "Give it a—"

His voice died abruptly as he felt the violent shiver that went through her. She jerked her head around to look at him, her eyes above his hand wide and shocked, full of alarm and outrage all out of proportion to what he'd done. He took his hand away. Quickly.

Claire inhaled sharply and moved away from him as if nothing had happened. "Before you all—" She paused and cleared her throat. "Before you all leave," she said again, her voice and manner as calm and cool as always, "there's just one more thing I'd like to say."

Five grown people groaned like children who'd been told recess was going to be delayed. The sixth stood behind her, wondering if he'd imagined that panicked look in her eyes.

"Relax," Claire said. "It's not another reminder or more last minute instructions, I promise. I just wanted to tell you all how much I appreciate the hard work you've been doing. I know I've been a little obsessive about this movie and—"

"Try a lot obsessive," Anna Markowitz, the script supervisor quipped.

"All right, a *lot* obsessive," Claire amended with a wry, self-deprecating smile. "And to make up for it, if only in a small way, I'm inviting you all to attend the charity bash Tara is throwing this Saturday night at Pierce's house. As my *guests*," she emphasized. "Spouses and significant others included. Although, I hope," she added, with a teasing look, "that you'll all have the good taste not to bring both at once. It'll be black-tie," she continued, raising her voice to be heard over the mild burst of laughter. "Dinner and dancing. And a silent auction for those of you who are interested. I'll even send a car for each of you so you don't have to contend with traffic. Any takers?"

Everyone said yes, of course. Tara Channing-Kingston's charity benefits were A-list all the way. She didn't give them often, for one thing, not like some other Hollywood hostesses, and invitations were a highly coveted commodity. Just being invited to one of her parties could improve a person's social standing and visibility in the movie industry. At the very least it was a chance to mingle with the movers and shakers. And at best . . . well, there were rumors that the details of more than one three-picture deal had been worked out on a cocktail napkin at one of Tara Channing-Kingston's parties.

Only Rafe didn't seem particularly excited. "I don't do benefits," he said to Claire while everyone else was heading out the door to the studio parking lot.

"No?" She flashed a quick look at him from the other side of the conference table. "Why not?"

"They're all a lot of industry hype and hot air, mostly," he said, staring at her bent head as she went around the table collecting crumpled napkins, crushed wads of paper and all the other stray bits of trash left after a day-long meeting. "You pay a couple of hundred dollars for a plate of overcooked pasta and a few nouvelle vegetables that wouldn't satisfy a rabbit. Maybe some creamed chicken if you're lucky." He picked up a wastebasket and started on the other side of the table, working his way toward her. "And all the money ends up being spent on decorations and entertainment rather than the charity."

"Well, I won't deny the hype and hot air. You can't get away from that in this town. But Tara always sets a fine table. She's doing Thai food this time, I think she said. Flying in some chef from San Francis—"

It startled her when he offered the wastebasket. She looked up at him quickly, dropped the trash she'd collected into the basket, and started back down the table in the other direction, gathering up file folders and notebooks as she went.

"You won't starve if you decide to come," she went on as if there hadn't been any interruption. "And all the proceeds are going directly to a maternity clinic in East L.A. to establish a prenatal health-care program. It's one of Tara's pet projects. She's been interested in it ever since her first baby was born prematurely and died. It was a long time ago, of course, but—"

"Claire." It was just that one word, spoken in his low, whiskey-rough voice, but it stopped her.

She clutched the stack of folders to her breast and lifted her head. "What?" she said, looking at him exactly the same way she had when he'd put his hand over her mouth.

Almost exactly, he amended.

There was no shock in her eyes now. And the panic had lessened to a sort of watchful apprehension. It reminded him, suddenly, of the half-wild kittens that were always prowling around their neighbor's barn when he was a kid. He'd trapped one of them once, wanting to see if he could turn it into a pet, and it had looked at him in just that way as he lay on his stomach on the floor of his room and tried to coax it to eat from his hand.

"Is it just me?" he asked softly. "Or are you afraid of all men?"

Claire's eyes registered instant indignation. "I'm not afraid of men."

"Then it's just me."

"I'm not afraid of you, either." She lifted her chin. "I don't know where you'd get such a ridiculous idea."

"Maybe it's the way you keep circling this table to keep it between us, as if you expect me to grab you and throw you down on top of it."

"That's absurd."

"Is it?"

"Totally," she snapped. "It's also annoyingly typical."

The way she said it reminded Rafe of that little cat again, and the way it had arched its back and hissed when he got too close. "Typical?"

"Why do men think that when a woman's not interested she's either afraid or frigid? Instead of realizing she's just fastidious about who she lets get next to her?"

"Shall we conduct a little test?"

"Test? What kind of a test?"

"You stand right there, without moving, while I come around the table."

Claire's eyes narrowed suspiciously. Warily. As if she expected some kind of trap. "And then what?"

"And then nothing. You just stand there, is all, while I come around and stand next to you. I don't think you can do it."

Her chin lifted another fraction of an inch and her body posture stiffened, as if she were going to refuse.

"I think you're afraid," he taunted.

Claire shrugged, lifting one shoulder in an elegant gesture of dismissal and disdain, and dropped the folders she was holding onto the table with a loud thud. "Suit yourself," she said, and began sorting through the papers as if she were totally alone in the room.

She could feel his heat as he came toward her, and she steeled herself against it, forbidding herself to move so much as a muscle in response. The only way to face him down and prove to him she wasn't afraid and wasn't interested was to show absolute, utter indifference. She waited until she could feel his chest touching her shoulder and his warm breath stirring the hair at her temple. And then she waited a full ten seconds more, just to prove her point.

"Satisfied?" she asked caustically, still without looking at him. Every nerve in her body was strung tight with tension, but she was determined to die before she'd let him know it.

Not by a long shot, Rafe thought, surprising himself. And he wasn't going to be satisfied, he realized, until he had her eating out of his hand. And purring. Just like that half-wild little cat.

But first she needed to realize she could trust him.

"You're a cool one, Claire Kingston. I'll give you that." His gravelly voice was low, amused and admiring, as heady as heated brandy. "But you're not as cool as you think. You're not as cool as anyone thinks. There's a volcano under that ice you keep yourself wrapped up in. I can see it in your eyes every time you look at me. And in the way you move your body under those prissy, buttoned-up clothes of yours. And under the soft skin just below your jaw, right—" he lifted his hand slowly and, very carefully, without touching her, pointed at the pulse throbbing above the high stand-up collar of her silk faille blouse "—there, beating against your skin like a drum. One of these days you're going to explode with all the passion that's locked up inside you. All you need is someone to give you a little push in the right direction. Someone to light the fuse for you. And I'm going to be that someone."

She turned her head slightly, tilting it to look up at him out of the corner of her eye. "Are you finished with your little analysis?"

Rafe smiled at the bite in her voice; the Ice Queen didn't give an inch. He nodded. "For now."

"Then get out of my way. I still have a lot of work to do before I can leave the office." She gave him a freezing look. "You, however, can feel free to leave any time."

He took the hint. "Oh, by the way." He paused on his way out. "What time will the car be around to pick me up tomorrow?"

"I thought you didn't do benefits?"

Rafe grinned at her from the doorway. "I changed my mind. What time?"

Claire thought briefly of telling him to forget it, that she was uninviting him, but that would have been far too revealing, making him think his bullying little test had affected her after all. Besides, she had invited all the others. The tabloids might try to make something of it if the director of her new movie was the only one who failed to show.

"The car will be there to pick up you up at seven-thirty. Sharp. And Rafe—" She waited until he turned to look at her. "Shave before you get dressed tomorrow night," she said with saccharin sweetness. "Otherwise you'll look like a two-bit gangster in that tux you have to buy. *If* you can find one on such short notice."

4

IT HAD PROBABLY just been a wild shot in the dark to get back at him for his "analysis" of her, Rafe thought as he settled into the back of the limousine she'd sent for him, but Claire had been right about the tux. He'd spent the better part of his Saturday morning being fitted for it, and it was only by the virtue of the very large tip he'd given the tailor at the very expensive store where he'd bought it, that he even had it to wear tonight. He could not, the salesclerk informed him, expect to walk in and be fitted off the rack.

Some echo of his frugal childhood, spent in hand-me-downs and other people's castoffs, told him it was ridiculous to spend so much on one suit of clothes, especially one he wasn't planning on wearing any more often than he absolutely had to.

But I'll be damned if I'm going to show up at that party looking like somebody's poor relation.

Claire's remark may have been a shot in the dark but it had unwittingly hit its mark, landing right smack-dab in the middle of Rafe's one insecurity. His background.

He'd grown up dirt-poor, in a small West Texas town not much different from the fictional Burley in *Desperado*, where his proud Mexican-American heritage was just another barrier to acceptance and success. His father had died when he was fifteen, making Rafe the head of the family when he was still too young for the responsibility. It was only his own fierce desire to succeed and his mother's indomitable will that had kept him in high school until he graduated. With six younger brothers and sisters to feed, clothe and educate, college had been out of the question. So Rafe had gone to work in the oil fields instead, sending most of his paycheck home each week.

He'd managed some higher education since then and life had added a lot of polish, but he still wasn't entirely sure which fork to use if there were more than two beside his dinner plate.

And that was the real reason he didn't "do" benefits or attend fancy Hollywood parties. He didn't feel comfortable at them. And he didn't want to risk looking like a fool.

He gazed down at the rich black fabric of his new tuxedo pants, at the shiny toes of the black eel-skin cowboy boots on his feet, at the plush luxury of the limousine that surrounded him, and wondered if that wasn't just exactly what he was doing anyway.

Making a damn fool of himself.

Over a pampered, privileged princess.

It had happened before.

The social lines in a small town like Flat Rock, Texas, were more sharply drawn than in most places and he'd been on the wrong side of them from the beginning. Oh, there'd been a few girls who'd been willing to step over the line—there always were, in any town—but never in public. And they'd always stepped back before there was any real risk to their social standing. But he'd been able to handle that. He was a walk on the wild side for most of them, and he'd known it. Reveled in it, sometimes.

There had been one girl, though, toward the end of his senior year of high school, who'd made him believe she was different. She'd dated him openly, tooling around town with the top down on the flashy red convertible her father had given her for her sixteenth birthday, holding hands with him at the Dairy Queen, inviting him to come swimming with her at the local country club despite all the small-town gossip and whispers of scandal. He'd fallen hard, offering his youthful heart and promises of a ring someday. She'd put off giving him an answer or offering anything in return until, finally, during the middle of a long, hot Texas summer she told him she didn't want to see him anymore. It wasn't until she left town a month later, without even a goodbye, that he realized she'd only been using him to maneuver her rich daddy into sending her to a fancy Dallas college.

There'd been other women since then, of course. So-called good women and not-so-good women, Anglo and Hispanic, from both ends of the social scale and just about everywhere in between. They'd taught him not to judge the entire sex by the actions of a spoiled few.

But those early lessons clung, coming back to haunt him at the most inconvenient times.

Like now.

CLAIRE WAS AT HER brother's palatial Beverly Hills estate by seven o'clock, dressed and coiffed and ostensibly ready to help her sister-in-law with any last-minute preparations before her guests arrived. But the truth was, she couldn't stand to be alone for another minute.

She needed people around her. Lots of people. And noise. Enough noise to keep her from thinking of the low, seductive sound of Rafe Santana's whiskey-rough voice when he told her that all she needed was someone to give her a push in the right direction. And that *he* was going to be that someone. The thought was almost as exciting as it was scary.

She stopped by the kitchen first, but Pierce's housekeeper, the redoubtable Mrs. Gilmore, had everything well in hand, harrying the catering staff in her usual no-nonsense style and looking daggers at anyone who even thought of interfering with any of her careful preparations.

Claire beat a hasty retreat and went upstairs.

She found Tara where she should have expected to, in the nursery suite that Pierce had had outfitted for visiting nephews, breast-feeding her new baby. Her husband—Claire's oldest brother, Gage—was reading one last bedtime story to two-year-old Beau. The little boy sat on his father's lap, his tousled blond head nestled against the fine knife-pleat tucks on the front of Gage's white dress shirt.

Tara looked up and smiled, motioning her sister-in-law forward, but Claire shook her head and backed out of the room. "I'll come back later," she mouthed, unwilling to intrude on such an intimate family scene.

She knew how hard Tara and Gage both worked to create the time for those precious moments in the hustle and bustle of their busy lives. And she knew how important the memory of them would be later, when the children were grown. Her own busy parents had left the creation of most of her precious moments to an English nanny.

She met Pierce and Nikki on the wide curving stairway leading down to the marbled foyer. They were hurrying up the carpeted steps with the stealth of sneak thieves, hand in hand and grinning at each other with the giddy happiness of newlyweds. It didn't take much imagination to guess where they were headed.

Claire stepped out of the way, standing close to the polished black walnut handrail, wondering if they would even notice her as they passed. They did, but only because Nikki glanced back over her shoulder to check the hall below. She stopped dead on the stairs. "Pierce," she said, yanking her husband to a stop beside her.

He looked around. "Oh. Hi, Claire. How's it going?"

"Just fine, thanks," she said, grinning at his nonchalance. Her brother had absolutely no sense of propriety when it came to indulging his rampant hunger for his wife. It was one of his many charms. "How's it going with you?"

"Until now—" he cast a teasing look at his blushing wife, who wasn't quite so nonchalant about being caught sneaking upstairs for a quickie by her sister-in-law "—I was doing just great." He leaned forward and kissed his sister on the cheek. "It's good to see you, Claire."

"It's good to see you, too." She returned the affectionate caress. "Both of you. But *why* am I seeing you? According to the production reports I saw the other day, shooting on *Made For Each Other* still has another two weeks to go, at least. Shouldn't you be in Toronto?" She lifted an eyebrow. "Working?"

"Aw, come on, Claire, lighten up," he drawled. "It's a party."

"We're only here for the weekend," Nikki said. "We'll be going back Sunday night." She gave her husband a look that dared him to dispute her. "*Won't* we, Pierce?"

He gave an exaggerated sigh, the epitome of the put-upon male. "Yes, dear."

Both women laughed, as they were meant to. "Well, carry on with what you were doing, then," Claire said. She waved toward the back of the house. "I'm off to take a look at what's been done in the backyard."

Pierce started up the stairs, ready to take her at her word, but Nikki was more reticent. She tugged on his hand, pulling him to a stop. "Pierce!" she whispered in a fierce undertone.

"What?"

She gave him a look that said he should know what, and tipped her head toward Claire.

"Claire doesn't mind. Do you— Aw, jeez," he said as Tara and Gage appeared at the top of the stairs. "So much for a clean getaway."

"I'm afraid you're too late to see the babies before they go to sleep," Gage informed his brother and sister-in-law as he came down the stairs with his wife at his side. The teasing expression on his ruggedly handsome face made it very clear he knew the nursery hadn't been their destination. "Chloe will be ready to eat again in three or four hours. And Beau always wakes up when his little sister does." He hooked his free arm through Nikki's as he passed her. "You can come up and see them then."

Pierce grimaced with comic dismay and presented his arm to his sister, silently offering to escort her. Laughing, she tucked her hand into the crook of his elbow and turned with him to follow the other three down the stairs.

RAFE STARED IN AMAZEMENT, forced to grin at the sheer absurdity of the sight that greeted him as the limousine drove slowly up the long, curved driveway. The structure looming up in front of him resembled nothing less than a Norman castle. The facade of the building was weathered gray stone, interspersed with sparkling leaded-glass windows and softened by the ancient ivy crawling up the walls toward the roof. A pair of stone lions, twice as big as the real thing, guarded the grand portal of the mansion. Two uniformed doormen stood at ease beside the lions, ready to spring into action the moment they were called upon to do so.

Motioning the chauffeur to stay where he was, Rafe took a second to trample down the anxiety he wouldn't ever admit to feeling. He passed a hand over his jaw, checking for stubble. He shot his cuffs, making sure the correct one-and-a-half inches of snowy Egyptian cotton showed beneath the sleeves of his jacket. He fingered the onyx studs in his starched shirtfront, making sure they were all there. And then he took a deep breath and reached for the handle of the car door.

The doormen snapped to attention as he stepped out of the limousine, reaching to sweep open the massive, double-wide front doors as Rafe mounted the smooth stone steps. He shook his head in amused disbelief, half-expecting a flare of trumpets to sound as he crossed the threshold. But it was the musical laughter of a woman that greeted him as he stepped into the foyer.

Claire's laughter.

He looked up toward the sound and found himself staring at a picture any self-respecting tabloid photographer would have sold his soul for. If he'd been directing a shot for the camera, Rafe thought, he couldn't have come up with a scene that would have epitomized the glamour of Hollywood any better than Claire and her family did coming down the wide, curving sweep of the stairs. Viewed individually, any one of them was a dazzling sight; together they produced enough star power to light up all of Los Angeles.

The two brothers were much alike in build and in bearing. Both of them were tall and broad shouldered, lean enough to appear elegant and at ease in their evening black and white. Pierce Kingston was the more polished of the two, with a halo of wavy blond hair, eyes of the same deep blue as his sister's and a face designed to make angels—and women—weep. Gage Kingston was darker, both in looks and in manner, with the amber eyes of a wolf and close-cropped hair of the same rich sable hue as Claire's.

The women were a study in contrasts. Tara Channing-Kingston was all lush, voluptuous opulence, with a tumbled cloud of red-gold hair and slanted aquamarine eyes that gave her a look of flirtatious seductiveness. Her creamy skin and magnificent bosom were displayed to excellent advantage by the portrait neckline of her full-skirted evening gown. Nikki Kingston was nearly as tall as her superstar husband, a sexy Amazon with long chorus-girl legs, sparkling pale green eyes and a feathery cap of supershort black hair. She was wearing a sleek column of red silk—high necked, long sleeved and slit halfway up her thigh on one side. And Claire was . . .

Rafe stifled a sigh of pure masculine appreciation.

Claire was a cool, sweet confection, as slender and elegant as a fairy-tale princess in a shimmering silvery blue sheath that left both arms and one shoulder beautifully bare. She wore her thick sable hair in its usual soft coil at the nape of her neck. The glitter of precious gems adorned her ears and circled the delicate bones of one wrist. The look on her lovely face was one he'd never seen before. It was soft, relaxed and utterly enchanting. Rafe couldn't tear his eyes away.

Claire felt his scrutiny like a warm caress against her cheek. She turned her head to see where the sensation was coming from, setting the diamond-and-pearl teardrops in her ears to twinkling in the light. Their eyes met.

And held.

The moment lasted for a second or two, perhaps three. Long enough for Claire to notice the way the superbly tailored jacket of Rafe's tuxedo fit across his broad shoulders. And how the snowy whiteness of his pin-tucked dress shirt emphasized the deep bronze glow of his skin. And the way his shiny black cowboy boots and his thick, shining black hair added an exciting touch of lawlessness to the formal elegance of his attire.

Long enough, too, to make her heart beat faster and her eyes heat with awareness.

And then Tara, ever the vigilant hostess, noticed the lone stranger standing in the entry hall. She disengaged herself from her husband's arm and hurried down the stairs and across the black-and-white marble tiles of the elegant foyer.

"I'm sorry," she said, gliding toward Rafe in a swirl of lavender lace and delicate perfume. "I didn't realize our guests were already arriving." She held out her hand in a simple gesture of warmhearted welcome. "I'm Tara Kingston."

"Rafe Santana." He reached out to take her hand in his. "The director for *Desperado*," he added helpfully when she couldn't seem to place him.

"Oh." Her lovely brow cleared. "You're Claire's director." She turned, smiling over her shoulder as she felt her husband's hand at the small of her back. "Gage, darling, this is Rafe Santana. He'll be directing Claire's new movie, *Desperado*. Remember? She mentioned it once or twice. Rafe, this is my husband, Gage."

The two men shook hands, eyeing each other in that way men have. Sizing each other up under the civilized guise of hospitality.

"And my brother-in-law, Pierce."

The ritual was repeated a second time with Claire's other brother.

"And his wife, Nikki."

"A pleasure," Rafe murmured as he clasped Nikki Kingston's slender hand in his.

She smiled at him.

"We were just on our way to the garden room to have a drink before all the craziness starts," Tara said when the introductions were over.

"Please, don't let me intrude," Rafe said quickly, before she felt compelled to invite him. "I'll find my way to the back—"

"Nonsense. Don't even think such a thing. We'd love to have you join us. It'll round out the numbers." Tara flashed a teasing sideways glance at her sister-in-law. "I'm sure that's what Claire had in mind when she invited you to come early. Wasn't it, Claire?"

Everyone turned to look at her, waiting for her answer. "Yes," Claire murmured, although she had no idea what she'd been thinking. She hadn't even been aware that she had invited him early, until now. "I guess it was."

"See, there?" Tara tucked her hand into the crook of Rafe's arm, steering him in the direction she wanted him to go. "You just come right along and tell us all about what's happening with you and Claire and *Desperado*. She's hardly said more than a word about it to any of us."

WELL, THIS ISN'T SO BAD, Rafe thought, relaxing a bit as he accepted a glass of champagne from his hostess's husband. His usual libation of choice was an ice-cold Lone Star, or a salt-rimmed margarita, but here, in this fairy-tale setting, with these beautiful people, a glass of champagne seemed exactly right.

"So," Pierce said, sitting down across from him on one of the three overstuffed sofas in the room. "How do you like working with our little dictator here?" He inclined his head toward his sister. "Have you popped her one yet?"

Rafe nearly choked on his champagne. "Have I *what?*"

Pierce grinned wickedly. "Popped her one." He curled his hand into a fist and set it, very gently, against Claire's raised chin to demonstrate.

She glared at him.

Rafe smiled, reminded of the affectionate wrangling he and his sisters and brothers indulged in when they were together. "I hadn't thought of using that particular approach," he admitted. "Is that how you usually handle her when she gets bossy?"

"Naw . . . I usually just do what she tells me."

"Because she's usually right," Nikki said from his other side.

Pierce reached out and cupped his hand around the back of his wife's neck. "She was right about you," he said, and pulled her toward him for a kiss.

"Pierce, please," Gage said, deadpan. "We have company."

"Oh, don't mind me." Rafe's gaze shifted to Claire as he spoke the next words. His voice lowered suggestively. "I don't mind a little healthy lust."

Claire returned his look for a long moment, mesmerized by the expression in his eyes. It made her think of explosions and passion and all those hidden emotions he'd accused her of having. *And* his low-voiced threat to be the one to bring them to the surface. She buried her nose in her champagne glass with a strangled little gasp, hoping no one would notice the sudden burst of color in her cheeks.

Claire's relatives exchanged significant glances.

"I understand you'll be going with Claire when she leaves for Texas tomorrow on the location hunt for *Desperado*," Gage commented.

Rafe had no trouble picking up on the subtext behind the other man's words, he had four sisters of his own. "She insisted," he said mildly. "And she's the boss."

Gage nodded curtly. "Just so you keep that in mind."

Rafe nodded his understanding, offering his silent assurance that Claire would be safe with him. Or, as safe as she wanted to be, at least.

"Well, now that that's settled..." Pierce said into the small silence that followed the exchange. He smiled at his wife. "Nikki and I have an announcement to make."

"I *knew* you'd come home for more than just this party," Tara said excitedly. She looked up at her husband. "Didn't I tell you?"

Gage put his hand on her bare shoulder. "You told me," he said, and looked at his brother. "Well?" he asked blandly, as if everyone hadn't already guessed. "Are we going to need more champagne to toast this announcement of yours?"

Pierce grinned like a pirate. "Hell, yes. More champagne for everyone. Except Nikki, that is. Give her another ginger ale." He took his wife's hand in his and lifted it to his lips. "She's carrying the next Kingston superstar," he announced grandly, beaming with pride as Nikki blushed with pleasure. There were hugs and hearty handshakes all around, and a few glad tears from the women. Rafe stood a little aside after he'd offered his congratulations, honored at being included but feeling just a bit out of place at such an intimate family celebration. News of a new baby was special. And private.

Or should be, he thought. Although, given the very public lives these people led, nothing was private for very long. Maybe that was why they shared the moment so easily.

"If there's any justice in this world, it will be a girl," Gage said, lifting his glass in a toast to his brother. He grinned evilly. "Payback for all the fathers you helped turn gray."

Everyone laughed at Pierce's comically horrified expression and lifted their glasses to drink.

"Excuse me." One of the white-coated caterer's staff appeared at the door as they prepared for another, more serious toast. "Mrs. Gilmore asked me to tell you that your guests are arriving."

Almost as one, the Kingstons put their glasses down on the glass-topped table. "It's show time," Pierce said, putting it into words for all of them.

Claire sighed. "Time to get to work."

THE LANDSCAPED GROUNDS of Pierce Kingston's lavish Beverly Hills estate twinkled with the hundreds of tiny white fairy lights that had been strung in all the trees. Music from the big band era, played by a live orchestra, drifted through the air. White-coated waiters passed deftly through the glittering crowd of party-goers around the lighted swimming pool, dispensing spicy Thai appetizers and champagne. Across the vast sweep of meticulously manicured lawn, under the billowing white tent set up over the tennis courts, the caterer's staff was busy putting the finishing touches on two dozen large, round dinner tables laid with white damask linens and sparkling china.

Rafe stood alone for the moment, leaning against one of the stone pillars that supported the balustraded terrace overlooking the pool. He sipped his second glass of champagne and watched Claire work the crowd.

In the past half hour, she'd exchanged pleasantries with Michael Douglas and his wife, had a fifteen-minute discussion with Susan Sarandon and Goldie Hawn about some organization called Women in Film, and air-kissed half-a-dozen agents, directors and various other Hollywood bigwigs.

"You really meant that about getting to work, didn't you?" he said, catching her just as she was making the move from one group to another.

"That's what Hollywood parties are for," she said, just a bit stiffly. "Why else do you think people go to so many of them?"

"Fun?"

"Networking." She took a small, quick sip of her champagne. "Contacts. Inside information. Who's in. Who's out. Who's doing what. Who's thinking of doing what. So, if you'll excuse me—" she moved as if to go by him "—I need to get back to work."

He stepped in front of her. "Look, I'm sorry for the remark I made about healthy lust. It was inappropriate in front of your family."

That wasn't what she was upset about. Not exactly, anyway. It was more her reaction to the remark that had her running scared. "Yes, it was," she said, and tried to step around him again.

He blocked her.

"I'm sorry for anything else I may ever have said to upset you, too."

"Rafe—"

"Come on, Claire. I said I was sorry. Have a little pity, woman."

"Pity?"

"I'm a fish out of water here. A round peg in a square hole. A social misfit." He smiled appealingly, trying for sheepish and harmlessly adorable now that he had her full attention. It wasn't one of his most convincing expressions. "You invited me to this shindig. It's your responsibility to see that I have a good time."

"You looked like you were having a pretty good time with Sharon Stone a few minutes ago."

He plastered a look of innocence on his face. "Is that who that was?" he said, elated that she'd noticed.

She stared up at him for a moment, torn between annoyance and amusement. Amusement won. "All right, come on." She signaled for a waiter to take her glass. "I'll show you how to power-mingle."

She tucked her hand into the crook of his arm the way she did with her brothers, unaware that it was the first time she'd ever voluntarily touched him. Rafe was aware of it, though. The feel of her small, elegant hand resting on his forearm burned through the fabric of his tuxedo jacket, all but searing the skin beneath. Afraid of calling her attention to what she'd done, he resisted the urge to reach over and cover her hand with his.

"Now, the first thing you've got to learn is to pick your target," Claire said. "We're headed that way." She nodded toward the opposite end of the pool. "Over there where Jon Peters"—the producer—"is talking to Arnold Schwarzenegger."

"Which one is our target?"

"Pick one," Claire invited.

"Schwarzenegger."

"Why?"

"He's a bigger target."

Claire laughed softly, delightedly, the way she had on the stairs, and squeezed his arm.

Rafe was entranced. "You should do that more often."

"Do what?"

"Laugh like that."

She glanced up at him, puzzled. "I laugh all the time."

Rafe shook his head. "Not like that."

"How, then?"

"You're more relaxed here. More spontaneous."

"It's my family," Claire said, surprised he had noticed a difference. She'd thought her acting skills were better than that. "I'm always more relaxed around them. I guess it's because they make me feel so safe."

"Safe?" he asked, thinking it was an unusual word for her to use.

"Loved," she said quickly, trying to cover her slip. "Cared for. Accepted. You kn— Oh, hello, Dennis.

Mary," she said, pausing to greet *Desperado*'s cinematographer and his wife. "Enjoying yourselves?"

"Yes, thanks," Mary Cleary said. "It's a wonderful party."

"I'm glad you're having fun." Claire smiled and moved on. "That was your second lesson in mingling," she said to Rafe as they threaded their way through the crowd that had congregated around the pool and cabana area. "How to meet and greet without slowing yourself down or losing sight of your goal." She exchanged a nod and a smile with fellow producer Sherry Lancing without breaking stride. "But," she added in a whisper, "you've also got to know when to stop and chat. Don. Melanie," she said warmly. "How are things going? Are you enjoying yourselves?"

Don Johnson saluted her with his glass of mineral water. "Tara throws a helluva party."

"I wanted to thank you again for the roses you sent," Melanie Griffith said in her breathy, little-girl voice. "It was a lovely gesture but it wasn't necessary. Honest."

"I know," Claire said, "but it made me feel better to send them."

"Roses?" Rafe asked after the couple had moved away to do some mingling of their own.

Claire grimaced. "There was a nasty little article about Don and me in one of the tabloids a few weeks ago."

"Yes, I vaguely remember seeing it." *The Ice Queen Comes Between Hollywood's Hottest Couple.* Just thinking about it annoyed the hell out of him; he didn't want to think about why that was. "So?"

"So I sent Melanie a dozen roses to say I was sorry."

"Sorry for what?"

"For the nasty little article."

"Why? It wasn't true." He paused for a moment, telling himself that it wasn't any of his business. That it didn't matter. That— "Was it?" he asked before he could stop himself.

Claire took her hand from his arm. "No," she said with chilly finality. "It wasn't."

"Isn't this a great party?" Pilar said, taking a breather from the action on the dance floor to sit down and talk to her brother for a few minutes.

"Great party," Rafe agreed morosely, his eyes focused on Claire as she conversed with director Ron Howard. She'd been ignoring him, assiduously, ever since he'd made that unfortunate remark about the tabloid article on her and Don Johnson. Hell, he knew better than to ask a stupid question like that! Claire Kingston wasn't the kind of woman who got involved with married men. As far as he could tell, she didn't get involved with men at all. Period. And, even if she did, it wasn't any of his business. Not yet, anyway.

"I can't believe all the movie stars that are here!" Pilar said. Even after nearly two years of working in Hollywood, Pilar was still as star struck as any fan. "I'm talking *big* movie stars. Huge. I sat at the same table at dinner with Denzel Washington and his wife, Pauletta.

She's gorgeous, by the way. And I actually had a conversation with Geena Davis while we were waiting to use the bathroom." She took a small sip of her drink. "Who'd you sit with at dinner? Rafe?" she prodded when he didn't answer. "What famous people were at your table?"

"Billy Crystal and his wife. Steven Spielberg. And ah—" he had to stop and think about it a minute "—that actress who played Cat Woman."

"Michelle Pfeiffer? You ate dinner with Michelle Pfeiffer and you're not even excited?"

Rafe shrugged. She hadn't been Claire, so he hadn't been interested. *God, what a sorry state of affairs!* His sister was right, he thought, as he sat there, scowling into his drink. Any normal, red-blooded man should have been thrilled to share a table with Michelle Pfeiffer. And all he had done was sulk because she wasn't Claire.

" . . . likes him very much."

"I'm sorry, Pilar." Rafe dragged his attention back to his sister. "What did you say?"

"I said I don't think Claire likes our leading man very much." She gestured with her drink. "That is Dax Wyatt with her, isn't it?"

Rafe looked where she pointed. It was indeed Dax Wyatt. And he was standing much too close to Claire, leaning in, holding her captive with the hand he had propped up against the stone pillar behind her head. She was turned away from him slightly, her face averted, her whole body unnaturally stiff. Any man with even a bare modicum of sensitivity would have already backed off a few feet and given her the space she so obviously wanted.

Claire had said he was a toad.

It looked as if Claire was right.

Rafe got to his feet, propelled by the blind, unreasoning rage of a man whose woman was being threatened, and stalked over to them. He put his hand on Dax Wyatt's shoulder, intending to whirl him around and plant a fist in his gut.

"What the—" Dax said, startled at being touched so abruptly.

Claire looked up at the sound, straight into Rafe's eyes. She read his intent clearly and her own eyes widened, pleading with him not to make a scene.

"Excuse me, Dax," he said, reining in his fury with a supreme effort of will. "But Claire promised me a dance before the party ends. I believe this is it."

5

THE BAND WAS PLAYING an old classic, a stately waltz in three-quarter time. The kind that, to be danced properly, required the partners to keep a proper distance. Rafe took her right hand in his left, put his other palm on the middle of her back just below her shoulder blades, and swung her into it. Claire clutched at the steely muscles of his shoulder and let him lead her where he would. It was soothing, she found, to be held and, yet, not held. They were almost arm's length apart, their bodies not touching yet connected, slowly revolving in time to the music.

Her frantic heartbeat started to slow, and the terrible panic began to recede after a few moments. Her hand gradually relaxed on his shoulder. Her skin warmed.

She looked up and found his eyes waiting for her. "Thank you," she murmured.

"You're welcome."

They made a few more graceful revolutions in total silence, their bodies turning as one, their eyes locked. Hers were wide and wondering, full of uncertainties and hesitations. His blazed with tender concern and more questions than she wanted to answer. She looked away.

"Are you all right?" Rafe asked.

"Yes." *Now.*

"What did he say to you?"

Claire shook her head. "Nothing, really. He was just being ... Dax."

"We'll get rid of him. Cancel his contract and get someone else to play Josh."

"No." She looked up at that, surprised that he would even suggest such a thing. Dax Wyatt had tested brilliantly for the part of Josh. "No, really. It's all right. He didn't do anything. He didn't even really say anything, when you come right down to it. He's just ..."

"An immature toad," he said, remembering her comment about the possibility of Dax Wyatt having matured since she last worked with him.

Claire surprised herself by actually smiling at that. "Yes. He's a toad. A talented toad but a toad, nonetheless." Her smile faded. "I should have handled it better. I *will* handle it better next time."

"Just pretend he's me," Rafe said, silently resolving that there wouldn't be a next time. Not if he had anything to do with it.

"Pretend he's you?"

"You don't seem to have any trouble putting me in my place when I cross the line," he said wryly.

Claire considered that for a moment. "That's because you're a gentleman." She realized, as she said it, that it was absolutely true. Deep down, where it really counted, he was a gentleman. And a gentle man. "You know how to take no for an answer."

Rafe grinned down at her. "Thank you. I think."

"I meant it as a compliment."

"I know. That's what has me worried. Back where I come from, when a woman tells you what a gentleman you are, the next thing you know, she starts talking about how much she trusts you and how safe she feels with you. What she really means is she's beginning to think of you as a brother." He pulled her just a bit closer to his chest. Not tightly but enough so that she could feel the hard muscle beneath the fabric of his jacket and shirt. "I'm not one of your brothers, Claire," he warned her. "Don't make the mistake of thinking I am."

"No," Claire said softly, staring up at him. "I won't."

The music stopped then, leaving them standing there in each other's arms.

"Why don't you let me take you into the house?" Rafe suggested. "The party's just about over, anyway. And you look beat. The other Kingstons can take care of whatever goodbyes are left to say."

Claire nodded. "Yes, all right. I'd like that. I am tired. And we do have that early flight to catch tomorrow."

"Today." Rafe glanced at his watch. "It's after one."

He led her off the dance floor and across the pool area, up the wide stone steps at the back of the pseudocastle to the second-floor terrace. It was dark and shadowed, hidden from the gaiety below by a balustrade draped with ivy and sweet-smelling bougainvillea. The chairs around the two glass-topped umbrella tables were blessedly empty.

"I think I'll just sit out here awhile," Claire said. "There's still bound to be a few guests inside. And it's so lovely and peaceful up here. You don't have to sit with me," she added, looking up at Rafe as she dropped into one of the cushioned wrought-iron chairs. "I'll be perfectly fine on my own."

"Are you trying to get rid of me?"

"No." And, incredibly, it was true. "I just thought you might want to go home and get some sleep before we leave tomorrow. Today," she corrected herself. "Whatever."

"I'll sleep on the plane."

"I envy people who can do that," she said. She dragged a second chair out from under the table with her foot and lifted her feet to the cushion. "Sleep on a plane, I mean. I never can."

"White-knuckle flyer?"

"No." She closed her eyes and leaned her head back. "I just can't sleep on a plane among all those strangers. With somebody else driving."

"You have a real problem with control, lady. You know that?"

"So I've been tol—" Her eyes flew open as she felt his hand slip under her crossed ankles. "What are you doing?"

"Just relax and close your eyes." He sat down in the chair she'd pulled out and put her feet in his lap. "I'm going to treat you to a little bit of heaven on earth." His teeth flashed in a grin. "Or, at least, that's what my mama used to say when I did this for her." He unbuckled the narrow straps of her high-heeled silvery blue evening sandals as if he'd done it a hundred times before, and slipped them off, carefully setting each one down on the floor beside his chair.

"You rubbed your mother's feet?" she asked as he began to squeeze her toes.

"Just about every night when she came home from work. She used to work in the cafeteria at the state hospital outside of Flat Rock. Even with the thick-soled shoes she wore, she still had problems after being on her feet all day. How's that feel?"

"Wonderful," Claire said, suppressing a moan as he rotated his thumbs against the balls of her stocking-clad feet.

She was a little embarrassed at first, sitting there in the dark with her feet in his lap and his strong hands stroking her. It seemed almost too intimate, somehow, and yet it wasn't at all, really. It was just...cozy. That's all. Comfortable. There couldn't possibly be anything sexual or threatening about it. Could there? He was just rubbing her feet.

He held a foot in each big, warm hand, his fingers resting lightly on her arches, his thumbs making small circles, working slowly up and down the length of each tender sole. He lessened the pressure over her sensitive insteps, pressing hard again over her heels, and then repeated the motion slowly, patiently, feeling the tension seep out of her with each knowing stroke of his thumbs. She moaned, finally, arching a foot into his caress as he massaged her Achilles tendon.

Rafe smiled to himself in the darkness and ran his hands up over her ankles and under the hem of her long silk dress to gently knead her calves. Women's calves always ached when they wore high heels for any length of time and Claire had been wearing hers for hours.

"Oh, God, that should be illegal," she groaned blissfully. "I've never felt anything so wonderful."

"Ahem!"

Claire jumped, trying to pull her feet off Rafe's lap, but he clamped his hand over her ankles, holding her where she was.

"Come on out," he called lazily to whoever was standing in the shadows behind her. "We're decent."

"Didn't sound very decent," Pierce said as he ambled out into the flickering light that reached the terrace from the decorated trees and the illuminated pool area below. "Sounded downright X-rated to me. It's a good thing it wasn't Gage who heard all that moaning and groaning," he said to Claire. "He'd be out here with a shotgun and a preacher."

"Oh, for heaven's sake, Pierce." Flushing with an embarrassment she hoped neither of them could see, she yanked her feet off Rafe's lap and put them onto the cold stone floor of the terrace. "He was just rubbing my feet."

"Ah." Pierce's tone carried a wealth of innuendo. "A man who can give a good foot massage can get anything he wants from a woman. Maybe I'd better go get Gage and that shotgun, after all."

Rafe laughed softly, as if in perfect agreement.

The sound sent shivers down Claire's spine. "Oh, shut up, both of you." She stood. "If this is going to turn into some kind of juvenile male bonding ritual where you start comparing techniques for getting women, I'm going inside."

"Tara and Nikki are in the nursery with the babies, if you're interested," Pierce told her. "Nikki said something about needing lessons in diaper changing."

"Good. I'm sure a conversation about diapers will be much more stimulating than listening to you two," she said, and headed inside.

"Well, I guess she told us," Rafe said, amusement in his deep voice. He stood. "And I guess I'd better get going, too. Do I just go out in front and ask for a car?"

"No need to rush off," Pierce countered. "The car will be there whenever you're ready." He stuck his hands into the pockets of his tuxedo pants and leaned his hips back against the ivy-covered balustrade as if he intended to stay awhile. "We always sit around the kitchen table and have coffee after a party. The ladies like to gossip about how it went. It's sort of a tradition around here, like champagne in the garden room before."

"I've intruded on enough of your private family traditions for one night."

"You'll hurt Tara's feelings if you don't. She told me to ask you to join us."

Rafe decided to meet that head-on. He liked to know exactly where he stood. "Why?"

"Well, Tara's a real tender-hearted woman and—" Pierce glanced at Rafe and lifted his shoulders in an easy shrug. "Not buying that, huh?"

"Oh, I don't doubt it for a minute. But that's not why you're asking me to join you."

"Well, hell." Pierce sighed theatrically. "Tara told me to be tactful about this but I guess you have a right to know. *I'd* want to know, if it was me. The ladies are planning to grill you." He flashed his famous megawatt, movie-star smile. "Very tactfully, of course."

"Grill me? Why?"

Pierce sobered, studying him for a moment before answering. "You're one of the few men Claire has ever shown other than a strictly professional interest in." He offered the information almost casually, but his blue eyes were intense and watchful as he gauged Rafe's reaction to it.

Rafe stared back at him steadily.

"You're also the first, and I mean the *very* first, she's ever brought home to meet the family, so to speak," Pierce continued, reassured by whatever it was he saw in the other man's dark gaze. "Kind of piqued our interest a bit."

His statement piqued Rafe's interest. Tremendously. "How few?"

"Two."

"Two?" Rafe echoed, finding that hard to believe.

"Unless she's got some secret life none of us know anything about, that's it. Two. And both relationships—if you can call them that—were lukewarm at best and never went anywhere, as far as any one of us could tell." His smile flashed again briefly. "And if you tell her I told you that, I'll deny it."

"Why the hell *are* you telling me this?"

"Because Claire's shown an interest, that's why. And because it doesn't look lukewarm this time. And because—" his blue eyes hardened in warning "—we want you to be perfectly clear about where the family stands on this."

"Do anything to hurt her and I'm dead meat."

"You got it." Pierce pushed himself away from the balustrade. "So, you going to risk upsetting Tara or will you join us for postparty coffee?"

Rafe matched Pierce's casual tone with one of his own. "I guess I can't take a chance on upsetting Tara."

"I wouldn't," Pierce said. "Gage can get real nasty with people who do that."

"Coffee it is, then," Rafe said, and moved to follow his host. He nearly tripped over Claire's shoes. Bending over, he picked the delicate high-heeled sandals up by the straps and followed Claire's brother into the house.

CLAIRE FOUND HER sisters-in-law right where Pierce had said they would be, in the nursery suite, fussing over the two youngest Kingstons.

"Speak of the devil," Nikki said, looking up from the baby on the changing table as Claire walked into the room. There was a teasing sparkle in her light green eyes. "We were just talking about you and that gorgeous hunk of yours. Where *have* you been hiding him?"

"He's not my hunk, he's my director. And I haven't been hiding him anywhere."

"Well, I certainly haven't seen him around here before. And I would have noticed a prime specimen like that if he was anywhere in the vicinity. He's almost as pretty as Pierce." She closed the last snap on the baby's flannel sleepers and picked her up. "Or this gorgeous young lady here," she said, lifting her niece up to nuzzle her tummy.

"You haven't been in a position to notice anything around here lately," Claire reminded her, bending down in answer to two-year-old Beau's tug on her dress. She picked him up when he raised his arms, settling him on her hip. "You've been out of town."

"So she has," Tara agreed. Her sweet smile was as teasing as Nikki's had been. "But I haven't. And I haven't seen him before, either."

"That's because he hasn't been anywhere for you *to* see. He's the director on my latest project. Period. Nothing else. No, Beau, darling, don't pull on Auntie Claire's earrings. It hurts." She held up her arm and waggled her diamond bangle back and forth in front of the little boy's eyes to redirect his attention. He began to twist it around her arm, trying to figure out how to get it off. "The only reason Rafe Santana was even here tonight," Claire continued, "is because I invited the entire staff of *Desperado* to be my guests as a thank-you for all their hard work."

"Yeah," Nikki said slyly. "But did you invite the rest of your staff to come early and have drinks with the family?"

"I didn't invite him to have drinks with the family." Although, unconsciously, that seemed to have been exactly what she'd done. "Tara did that."

"Well, I couldn't very well just leave him standing in the foyer, could I?" Tara said with exaggerated innocence.

"Well, no but—"

"And besides," Nikki said, "it wasn't Tara who spent the whole evening exchanging hot-eyed glances with tall, dark and handsome."

Claire's chin lifted. "I did not ex—"

"Knock, knock." Pierce's voice came from behind the door. "Is everybody decent? Can we come in?"

All three women started guiltily. "We were coming down in a minute," Tara said. "Just as soon as we got Chloe and Beau bedded down again."

"That's okay," Pierce said as he entered the room carrying a tray full of cups and saucers. "We decided to come up, instead." Gage followed with another tray holding a full pot of coffee, cream and sugar. Behind him was Rafe, Claire's high-heeled sandals dangling from his hand.

He held them out to her on a crooked finger. "You left these out on the terrace."

"I hope that's all she left out there," Gage said as he put his tray down on the child-sized nursery table.

Claire gave her bother a freezing glare and then, to her horror, blushed beet red.

Beau patted his aunt's cheek. "Hot," he said, and then chortled gleefully when everyone laughed. "Hot, hot, hot," he repeated, hoping to elicit another round of laughter.

It was Rafe who came to her rescue. "Aren't families wonderful?" he commented dryly, redirecting everyone's attention from Claire to himself. "Here, you take these." He extended the shoes toward her. "And I'll take the budding comic there."

"I don't know if he'll go to you," Claire said doubtfully. "He can be a little shy some—"

Beau threw himself forward in that sudden, lurching way small children have.

Rafe dropped the shoes and reached out, scooping the toddler up against his chest before Claire could let go. Her arm was caught, pressed against Rafe's hard chest by the soft little body of her nephew. The back of his hand was pressed against her breasts.

They both froze for an instant, standing there in an almost embrace, staring at each other, enmeshed in a sudden warm veil of intimacy. Claire's nipples hardened beneath of silk of her dress. The muscles in Rafe's chest tightened and flexed. Desire flowered softly between them, full-blown and fierce on Rafe's part, newly budded and fragile on Claire's. The feeling was palpable, alive to everyone in the room. Claire and Rafe swayed closer, yearning toward each other.

The child between them began to squirm.

Claire gasped softly, dismayed, and started to back away. Rafe instinctively resisted her move, tightening his arm around the little boy as if that would bring the woman he wanted closer.

"Down," Beau demanded, his lower lip beginning to quiver dangerously.

Rafe recovered himself then, dragging his eyes away from Claire's, lifting Beau slightly so she could slide her arm free. "There, now," he said cajolingly, bouncing the toddler slightly in an effort to forestall his incipient tears. But Beau had had enough. He looked up at the strange man who held him and began to whimper.

"Here, I'll take him," Gage said, quickly stepping into the breach. "Come see your ol' man, son. Look." He turned toward his wife. "There's mama."

And, suddenly, everyone except Rafe and Claire was gathered around the makeshift coffee table, cooing over what a good boy Beau Kingston was and busily issuing requests for coffee with varying amounts of cream and sugar. Rafe and Claire were left standing on one side of the room, as alone as it was possible for a couple to be in a room full of interested relatives.

He wanted to touch her. The soft alabaster skin, still warm with her blushes. The sable hair, falling down on one side where her nephew's hands had pulled at it. The bitten-cherry lips, tender and trembling. She was looking down, twisting the diamond bracelet around and around on her wrist.

She'd only ever felt like this one time before, trembling and eager and afraid all at the same time. She didn't trust the feeling. She didn't trust any feeling, really, except those she felt for her family. Feelings were fickle things, easily manufactured, easily changed, easily mistaken for something they weren't. And this one, especially, was treacherous, stirring yearnings for things she wasn't really sure she wanted, for things that had only ended up hurting her before.

"Claire," Rafe murmured achingly, too low for anyone else to hear. "Claire, look at me."

She looked up, meeting his gaze with a quick, sliding glance that never quite connected.

Rafe sighed. He couldn't touch her now, not with her family standing twelve feet away, pretending not to notice. He couldn't turn her chin up and demand that she look him in the eyes. Couldn't ask her why the thought of his passion, and her own undeniable response to it, made her so suspicious and afraid.

"I think I'd better be going," he said, knowing nothing would be resolved that night, in that room.

She nodded, not even attempting the polite fiction of urging him to stay for coffee.

"Walk me to the front door?"

Claire hesitated.

He glanced over the people clustered around the coffee tray. "They'd think it was strange it you didn't," he warned, using the only means of persuasion he had at his disposal. "And they're going to jump all over you with a hundred questions if you're still in this room after I leave."

It was that, more than anything, that persuaded her. She nodded. "I'm going to walk Rafe out," she said to her family. "And then I'm going to bed."

She had a room in her brother's house—they all did—stocked with duplicates of all her toiletries and a few wardrobe basics. She would sleep here tonight, get up before anyone else to avoid those questions Rafe had mentioned, and stop by her own house for her luggage on the way to the airport in the morning.

They left the nursery together, after Rafe had acknowledged a round of polite goodbyes from her family, and walked down the sweeping staircase side by side, silently, without touching. The grand foyer below was bathed in shadows, the black-and-white marble tiles patterned with soft lozenges of light shining from upstairs.

Claire was stiff with anxiety by the time they reached the bottom step, wondering if he would try to kiss her, wondering if she would let him.

She hadn't let anyone for a long time.

She hadn't wanted anyone to for an even longer time.

"I won't if you really don't want me to," Rafe said, standing back a bit as she entered a short series of numbers into the security panel by the massive front door.

She didn't look at him. "Won't what?"

"Kiss you good-night. Although," he added casually, "I'd advise you to pluck up your courage and get it over with."

She did look at him then, turning to glance over her shoulder. The expression in her blue eyes was a brave parody of her usual cool self-possession. "And why is that?"

"Because we both know it's going to happen eventually. And you know what they say, anticipation is always nine-tenths of everything, and nothing is ever as bad, or as good—" that little reminder was for himself "—as you think it's going to be. If I don't kiss you now, you'll just end up worrying about it all night long and wondering when I *am* going to kiss you. And then you won't get any sleep at all and you'll be irritable and groggy tomorrow on the plane. You might also consider that, with both your brothers upstairs, I won't dare do anything more than kiss you. Which might not be the case later. All in all, I don't think you're going to find a better—" *or safer*, he thought, remembering the remark she'd made earlier "—occasion for our first kiss." He forced himself to grin. "Besides, I can guarantee you'll like it."

"And what if I don't happen to want you to kiss me? Ever?"

"But you do." His voice changed to a gravelly, seductive whisper that floated down over her shoulder to caress her ear. "Don't you, Claire?"

She hesitated for a moment, her hand on the curved door handle, thinking hard, trying to judge the reality of her feelings. *Did* she want him to kiss her? Really? "Yes," she admitted, more to herself than to him. "Yes, I do."

"Well—" he deliberately made his voice light, playing down the emotion of the moment "—turn around then, so I can plant one on you."

He waited for what seemed like forever for her to do as he asked. And then, suddenly, she was looking up at him, her extraordinary blue eyes glistening like jewels in the dim light. She seemed so small and vulnerable to him, standing there in her elegant silk dress and diamonds, with her feet bare and soft tendrils of sable hair trailing over one shoulder. Her expression was guarded and wary, more like that of a child waiting to be punished than a woman waiting to be kissed.

Rafe wanted to reach out and take her in his arms. Not in passion but in tenderness. To soothe and reassure and protect her from whatever it was that was making her quake at the mere thought of being kissed. He was beginning to have his suspicions about what "it" was, and those suspicions weren't pleasant.

"They make me feel safe," she'd said of her family.

And he'd thought it a strange thing for her to say.

"You're one of the very few men Claire's ever shown an interest in," Pierce had said of him.

Which was stranger still.

Claire Kingston was a beautiful woman. Talented. Creative. Passionate. And she was in a business that attracted handsome, talented, creative, passionate men. The idea that none of them had ever started a fire in her was so ridiculous as to be absurd. *Unless* what he was beginning to suspect was true.

In which case, the Ice Queen routine of hers was an act. Camouflage. Protective coloring. Was he the only one who saw through it to the frightened woman beneath? The only one who suspected the reason she'd assumed the frosty persona in the first place?

"If you're going to do it, then do it," Claire snapped. Her nerves were stretched taut with the waiting—and the war going on inside her. Wanting his kiss. Yet dreading it, too. This kind of ambiguity was what had gotten her into trouble before. "I'd like to get some sleep before I have to get up and catch that plane in the morning."

Rafe smiled, pleased. She was frightened but she wasn't cowed. He took a step toward her.

She flinched but held steady.

"Close your eyes, Claire," he murmured huskily.

Claire's eyes remained stubbornly open.

"All right," he said, sighing. "Have it your way." And then, very slowly, with his hands held deliberately at his sides, Rafe bent his head to kiss her.

His lips touched hers lightly, delicately, like a butterfly landing on a flower, exerting no pressure, using no coercion or constraint to keep her from backing away. He could feel the tautness in her, the tension, but she held very still, neither advancing nor retreating from his careful caress. He increased the pressure of his mouth on hers, ever so slightly, ready to back off at the first sign of withdrawal.

But Claire didn't move. She hadn't thought a man's lips could be so soft. Nor his kiss so gentle. But his mouth on hers was as sweet and nonthreatening as the baby kisses Beau pressed against her cheek. Her eyes drifted closed and she relaxed a tiny, almost infinitesimal degree. She leaned forward just slightly, her mouth exerting a delicate, testing pressure against his.

Every nerve in Rafe's big body tightened in response. He stuffed his hands into his pants pockets to keep from reaching for her and took the kiss a shade deeper.

She felt his mouth open on hers, felt his lips brush back and forth in a sliding caress, but there was still no demand. No pressure. No force. Her lips began to heat and tingle. They softened and parted slightly, unconsciously inviting more intimate contact.

Rafe's hands curled into fists inside his pockets as he accepted her invitation. He opened his mouth a bit wider over hers, letting his tongue glide over the seam of her lips, making the kiss wetter. Hotter. Patiently teasing and tantalizing until her own latent desires would push her to go further. And driving himself crazy in the process.

Kissing Claire wasn't as good as he had anticipated. It was better. Much, much better. The taste of her was intoxicating. The feel of her mouth moving so shyly against his was maddening. The delicate pressure of her lips was more intense, more pleasurable, than any of the deep tongue-kisses he'd shared with other women.

And he didn't know how much more he could take without losing control.

He wanted to wrap his arms around her, pull her slender body to his and crush her small, soft breasts against his chest. He wanted, desperately, to plunge his tongue between her perfect lips and ravage the hot, sweet silkiness of her mouth. But he held himself back, knowing he couldn't give in to his desires until he'd coaxed Claire to give in to hers.

He wondered if a man could die of frustration.

And then her tongue snaked out softly, delicately, hesitantly, and touched his. Groaning, Rafe followed it with his own as it disappeared back between her lips, unable to deny himself just one sweet taste of what she unconsciously offered.

And then he lifted his head and stepped back from her.

"Good night, Claire." His voice was gruff with wanting. His eyes were dilated with passion. His body was rock hard and throbbing. "I'll see you at the airport in the morning."

He reached for the curved handle on the door and yanked it open, desperate to get away before he gave in to the stunned look of nascent desire in her wide jewel-bright eyes. If he gave her the kiss he wanted to give her, the kiss she had unwittingly asked him for, he'd scare her to death. He knew instinctively that she wasn't ready for the full force of his unleashed passion, and he couldn't continue to kiss her without giving in to it.

He hurried out the front door, past the stone lions that guarded it, down the wide smooth steps, and disappeared into the waiting limousine without a backward glance.

Claire stood in the open doorway of her brother's house with her fingertips pressed to her tingling lips and watched the car until it passed through the gates at the end of the long, curving driveway. She wondered if she'd just taken the first scary step on a journey she'd never intended to take again. And wondered, too, why the thought of taking that journey wasn't quite as terrifying as she'd always thought it would be.

6

THE ICE QUEEN WAS BACK the next morning, sitting primly in the seat next to Rafe on a plane bound for Lubbock, Texas. She had barricaded herself behind her image with a vengeance: sensible pumps; buttoned-up, touch-me-not designer suit; flawless chignon; perfect, impeccable makeup; and a manner so brisk and chilly a man could get frostbite just looking at her.

Rafe was disappointed at her all-out retreat into her protective persona but not particularly surprised. He'd learned that one step forward and two back was about par for recovery from any kind of traumatic experience—be it physical, emotional or spiritual. In Claire's case, he thought, covertly studying her profile as she hid a yawn and pretended to read the contents of the open folder on her tray table, it was probably all three.

Rape had to be a pretty all-encompassing trauma for a woman.

After his conversation with her brother last night and the kiss he'd shared with Claire, Rafe was more convinced than ever that that's what had happened to her. She hadn't been merely hesitant or apprehensive at the thought of kissing him, or even simply displaying a smart woman's instinctive caution with a new man.

And it hadn't been nervous excitement that had caused her mouth to tremble beneath his. It had been fear.

Primal, gut-wrenching fear.

But she'd kissed him in spite of it.

It gave him hope. Hope that, one day soon—before he went out of his mind with frustration!—she'd let him do more than just kiss her. That she'd *invite* him to do more. And that she'd participate wholeheartedly and heatedly.

The woman at the twenty-four-hour rape crisis center he'd called after he got home from the Kingston benefit had given him hope, too.

"Not knowing the circumstances, I can't say anything for sure, of course," the woman had said. "But it sounds like your perceptions could be accurate, that she was raped. If she was and you're the first man she's shown any real interest in since then, well...take it very slow is the best advice I can give you. Don't push her into anything. See if you can get her to talk about it. That always helps. And encourage her to get counseling. Even at this late date, it could help her deal with her feelings about the experience. But, above all," she'd reiterated, "don't make any sexual demands or push her to respond to you. Let her be the one to lead the way and set the pace."

Rafe fully intended to follow the woman's advice. To a point.

He wouldn't push or pressure Claire. There would be no demands. He would simply be there every time she turned around. Tempting her. Teasing her. Letting her get used to the smell and feel and *presence* of him. Guiding her gently in the right direction until she trusted him enough to give in to the passion locked away inside her.

She already trusted him more than she knew. A few moments ago, she'd fallen asleep beside him—this woman who'd told him she couldn't sleep among strangers, with somebody else doing the driving. Her elegant hands were lax in her lap, her head tilted at an awkward angle against the back of her seat.

Smiling tenderly, Rafe carefully plucked her Mont Blanc pen from between her fingers and put it on the tray table. Then he lifted the armrest between them, pushing it out of the way between the seat backs, and slipped his arm behind her shoulders. She murmured sleepily, as if in protest, and shifted restlessly. Rafe held his breath, expecting her to wake up and object to his familiarity, but she only snuggled her cheek over his heart as she settled against him, as trusting as a kitten in familiar hands. Her hand rested on the soft black shirt fabric over his flat stomach, just above his silver concha belt buckle. Rafe covered it with his, pressing it against him, and closed his eyes. A small smile of satisfaction curved his hard lips as he drifted off to sleep himself.

" . . . CAPTAIN HAS TURNED on the seat belt sign for our descent into Lubbock airport. Please stow your tray tables and return your seat backs to their full upright position. Any carryon luggage you may have used during the flight should be . . ."

The metallically distorted sound of the flight attendant's voice as it came over the loudspeaker roused Claire from a deep sleep. It roused Rafe, too, but he remained motionless, with his eyes closed, waiting to find out what Claire would do. He felt her start to sit up and then stiffen against him, as if she'd just realized what and who she was using as a pillow. He heard her gasp softly and could almost see the consternation on her lovely face as she considered her options.

Glancing up at his face to make sure he was asleep, Claire bit her lip and slipped her hand out from under his, stealthily, a millimeter at a time. Then she grasped the thick wrist draped over her shoulder in two fingers and lifted it, ducking her head out from under his arm at the same time. A moment later, she had rescued her Mont Blanc, gathered the papers on her tray table into a tidy pile, and was nudging the man beside her with her elbow.

"Rafe, wake up," she said briskly. "We're getting ready to land."

"Hmm?" Rafe pretended to come awake slowly. He rolled his big shoulders and stretched his arms out in front of him, rubbing against Claire in the process.

She didn't even flinch.

"Was I asleep long?" he asked.

"Most of the trip, I guess," Claire mumbled, reaching down for the briefcase under the seat in front of her. She snapped it open on her lap. "I didn't really notice."

"Worked all the way, huh?" Rafe asked, watching as she placed the folder into one accordion slot and slipped her pen under the leather loop specifically made to hold it. Even her briefcase was neat and tidy, he noted.

"Mmm-hmm." She snapped the case closed and put it back under the seat. "Planes are a great place to get a little work done."

If that's the way she wanted to play it, Rafe thought, then that's the way they would play it. For now. He wouldn't even mention the faint rippling impression on her soft cheek, caused by the button flap of his shirt pocket.

"WHAT TOWN IS THIS?" Claire asked, squinting at the map in the fading light as they approached yet another small West Texas burg.

Rafe didn't have to look at the sign welcoming them to town. "Ropesville." He glanced over at her. "What do you say we stop?"

Claire lifted her head to look out the car window at the passing scenery. "No, it's not right," she said, shaking her head. "Too big. Too busy." She went back to studying the map spread out across her lap. "I think we need to get off this road onto something less traveled. More remote. Take the next left we come to." She lifted the map closer to her face, trying to see it better. "It should be route 41."

Rafe pulled into the parking lot of the next motel he saw.

Claire looked up from the map as the car came to a stop. "What are you doing? Why are we stopping?"

"In case you haven't noticed, the reason that map is getting so hard to read is because the sun is almost down. I think it's time we stopped for the day."

"But—"

"But nothing," Rafe interrupted. His patience, tried by a long day of dealing with the Ice Queen at her most frosty and off-putting, was nearly at an end. "We've been driving around in circles now for—" he glanced at his watch "—nearly six hours, crisscrossing every blasted square inch of this godforsaken desert. I've had less than five hours' sleep in the last thirty-six, one of which was a catnap in a cramped airplane seat. And all I've had to eat is that rubber omelet they served us on the plane this morning and a hamburger from Dairy Queen. I'm tired and I'm hungry. I want a hot shower, a cold beer and a steak dinner with all the fixin's. In that order. And then I want to call it a day and sack out for a solid eight hours. I should think you'd be ready to call it a day, too." He fixed her with a dark-eyed stare, taking in the sheer, unruffled perfection of her. She looked as fresh and unwrinkled as when they'd started out that morning. For some reason that annoyed the hell out of him. "Or doesn't the Ice Queen of Hollywood have the same human frailties as the rest of—" He broke off at the hurt look that suddenly filled her eyes. "What?"

Claire looked away. "You're right," she said, staring down at the map. "It's been a long day." She began folding it—or trying to. Why was it, she wondered, that maps never refolded as easily as they unfolded? "We're both tired and—"

He reached across the seat to touch her and then, thinking better of it, curled his fingers over the edge of the map instead, halting her fumbling efforts to deal with it. "I didn't mean to snap at you," he said, feeling like a prize heel for putting that wounded look on her face. It wasn't anything she'd done that had him so testy, anyway; it was being so close to his old stomping grounds that had really put him out of sorts. He released the map. "I'm sorry."

Claire shook her head again. "There's nothing to be sorry about," she murmured, staring at the map through a sudden, inexplicable haze of tears. She opened her eyes very wide, a trick she'd learned to keep the tears from falling. "You're right about stopping. And I . . ." The trick wasn't working. "Damn," she said softly, turning her head to stare out the window. Her hands clutched the edges of the map, crushing it.

"Aw, Claire . . . for God's sake . . ." Rafe watched, horrified, as the first fat tear trickled down her averted cheek. "Claire, honey. Don't do that," he said, as desperate and helpless as any man in the face of a woman's tears. "We don't have to stop now if you don't want to," he wheedled, willing to offer anything in an effort to end the waterworks. "We can keep driving for as long as you want."

Another tear followed the first. She wiped it away with the palm of her hand, like a child. "Th-that's not the reason," she said, disgusted with herself and her sudden weakness. She'd been able to cry on cue since she was four years old, but she couldn't seem to make herself *not* cry now. It was humiliating.

"Then what is the reason?" Rafe asked.

She shook her head. "It's nothing. I'm sorry." She wiped at her cheek again. "I don't know what's the matter with me ... acting like this, I—"

Rafe couldn't stand it another minute. He reached out and cupped her cheek in his palm, gently turning her around to face him. "Tell me," he commanded softly.

Claire stared at him for an aeon-long second, her blue eyes jewel bright and sparkling beneath the shimmer of tears, her lush bottom lip trembling, her ivory cheek soft and wet against his palm.

Rafe wanted to kiss her tears away. Tenderly. Slowly. And, oh, so sweetly. And then he wanted to kiss her perfect lips until they trembled in passion rather than unhappiness. "Tell me," he murmured, forcibly restraining himself from doing either.

"I *hate* that nickname," Claire burst out passionately. "I've *always* hated it. But I hate it even more when you say it."

"What? The Ice Queen?"

She nodded against his hand. "It makes me sound so cold and...and unfeeling and..." And she wasn't sure that it wasn't true. Even now, when her feelings seemed to be choking her, she wasn't sure.

"Then I won't say it," Rafe vowed. "And I'll beat up anybody else who does." He lifted his other hand, cupping her face between his palms, and tenderly wiped away the last of her tears with his thumbs. "Okay, now?"

She sniffled a bit and nodded. "I'm sorry for acting like such an id—"

"No." He touched a thumb to her lips. "I'm sorry for making you cry. It won't happen again." *I hope.* It took every ounce of willpower he had, but he made himself take his hands away from her face and sit back. "What do you say we get ourselves a couple of rooms at this motel?" he suggested. "Then we'll shower and change and go find ourselves two of the biggest, juiciest steaks in Ropesville."

Feeling strangely bereft at his withdrawal, Claire had to force herself to respond in the same lighthearted manner. "Do you think we could make one of those steaks a vegetarian plate?" she asked. "I don't eat meat."

"I DOUBT THIS PLACE actually has anything called a vegetarian plate on the menu," Rafe said forty-five minutes later when they were settled across from each other at a table in Sam's Steak House. "But I know for a fact they have pinto beans, baked potatoes and fried okra because they all come with the steak. You can probably get a salad, too, if you ask real nice."

"How do you know what comes with the steak?"

It amazed him that he actually considered lying to her. He hadn't experienced the cowardly impulse to lie to a woman about his origins since he'd learned that not all women judged a man by who his granddaddy was or how much money his family had.

"I grew up less than fifty miles from here," he said. "Ropesville was where you brought your date if you wanted to impress her. It had the closest movie theater, a bowling alley and the nicest restaurant for miles. Outside of the Flat Rock Country Club, that is," he added sourly. "But that was for members only."

"And I take it you weren't a member?"

Rafe snorted. "Not hardly," he said bluntly, to make up for his impulse to lie. "My family came from way on the other side of the tracks. Our kind wasn't welcome within a hundred feet of the place except as grounds-keepers and kitchen help," he added, wondering what a woman who'd undoubtedly never been denied entrance anywhere would make of that.

She didn't seem to make anything of it. "Does your family still live there?" she asked instead. "In Flat Rock?"

"My mother does—in the same house I grew up in—with my youngest brother, Matteo. Until he leaves for Texas Tech next fall, that is. And my oldest sister, Inez, still lives there, too. She married a local rancher. My second sister, Mercedes, and her husband live about a hundred miles from here as the crow flies, just outside of Brownfield. They run a flying school and an airplane maintenance business out of the local airfield there."

"How many brothers and sisters are there?"

"Seven, including me. Inez, Mercedes, Ramona—she's a public defender in Dallas," he said with obvious pride and affection. "Pilar, Luis—who's a sophomore at Tech—and Matteo."

"And your father?"

"My father died in an oil field fire when I was fifteen."

"Oh." The way he said it let her know the subject was still painful. "I'm sorry."

"Yeah," he said gruffly. "So am I."

The waitress came with their drinks then. An ice-cold Lone Star beer for Rafe; a Texas-sized quart glass of iced tea for Claire. She took their orders then, too, hardly batting an eyelash when Claire requested a steak dinner without the steak.

"I suppose you're going to see your family while you're here?" Claire said when the waitress had gone.

Rafe sighed. "I suppose." If he got this close without stopping to visit, his mother would have his head on a platter.

Claire looked at him curiously. It sounded as if his family was a close-knit one; she thought he would have jumped at the chance to visit with them. "Don't you want to?"

"Oh, sure, I want to. It's just that . . ." He shrugged, picking at the label on his beer bottle with his thumbnail. "My mother will make a big production out of it. The prodigal son returns and all that. She'll want to call all the relatives for two hundred miles around, kill the fatted calf and have a big family party."

"So?" Claire couldn't understand his reluctance. If her mother had wanted to throw a party just to welcome *her* home, she would have been tickled pink. But Elise Gage didn't have much use for parties that didn't serve some function beyond the merely social. "It sounds nice."

"Yeah." Rafe winced inwardly, thinking of the party he'd been to at her brother's home the night before. And the way it would compare to one at his mother's. "Nice."

"I think you should let her do it," Claire said as the waitress set their salads down in front of them.

Rafe grinned ruefully. "Once she finds out I'm coming, I won't have much choice," he said, and picked up his fork.

The lettuce was iceberg instead of Bibb or endive, but it was fresh and crisp and served on ice-cold plates. The tomatoes smelled like tomatoes were supposed to smell but usually didn't. Claire ate with real enjoyment, savoring the vinegary tang of the house dressing, the sharp bite of the slender rings of red onion and the crunchiness of the homemade croutons. A basket of Texas Toast was served with the salads, thick slices of sourdough bread lavished with melted butter and garlic and roasted on a grill.

"I didn't think you had it in you," Rafe commented after they'd eaten several minutes in dedicated silence.

Her mouth full, Claire merely lifted an eyebrow in silent inquiry.

He gestured at her nearly empty salad plate with his fork. "You're really packing it in there."

Claire swallowed. "You may have had a hamburger this afternoon," she reminded him, "but all I had were a couple of French fries and a diet Coke."

"I thought that's because you were on some crazy diet. If you'd mentioned before that you were a vegetarian, we could have stopped at a grocery store somewhere and picked up some fruit or something."

"I didn't want to make a fuss."

So speaks the woman, Rafe thought, who had no trouble making a great deal of fuss where one of her movies was concerned. He shook his head at the vagaries of the feminine psyche. "So you go hungry instead." He snorted in amused disgust. "Well, tomorrow morning," he said, in a tone that brooked no argument, "we'll pick up a cooler before we hit the road and stock it with fruit and soft drinks. We should've done it before we left Lubbock. Better for both of us than greasy hamburgers. Ah . . . here's my steak." His eyes lit up in anticipation, making him look boyish and eager. "I haven't had a decent piece of beef since the last time I was in Texas," he told Claire as he set his knife and fork into the oversized slab of meat.

Claire let him eat the first few bites in blissful silence, waiting until he seemed to have satisfied his initial craving for the blood-rare beef. Once he'd settled down to merely eating, as opposed to savoring the gastronomic nuances of every mouthful, she spoke up.

"Since you grew up around here, you must have a pretty good idea of the characteristics of all the little towns in the area," she said, tacitly questioning the way he'd let her direct them up and down and around the countryside, looking for the perfect Burley.

"Not really," Rafe said, knowing very well what she was getting at. "I left home a couple of months after I graduated from high school." Right after Laura Lyn Parker got what she wanted from her daddy and dumped him in favor of S.M.U. "And I haven't been back for any length of time since then. These little towns change real fast, especially when the economy's as unstable as it has been for the past ten or twelve years."

"Where'd you go? When you left high school, I mean?"

"Not far, at first. I got a job in the Midland oil fields, then moved on to Houston and finally out onto a rig in the Gulf."

"How'd you get from an oil rig in the Gulf of Mexico to directing movies in Hollywood?" she asked, fascinated by this glimpse into his past. It was so different from anything she'd known growing up, she was consumed with curiosity about him.

"A documentary film company was doing a piece about life on a deep-sea oil rig. I was still just a kid at the time—not quite twenty-three—and making movies, even if they were only documentaries, seemed a whole lot more glamorous and exciting to me than working on an oil rig in the middle of the Gulf. I sort of attached myself to the film crew and when they left—" he shrugged and forked up a bite of baked potato dripping with sour cream "—I left with them as a gaffer's assistant. Then the project wrapped and I found myself flat broke in La La land and looking for another job."

"Is that when you went to work as a stuntman?"

Rafe nodded. "Yeah. It seemed more exciting than hauling lights and camera equipment around." *Besides paying a helluva lot better than being a gaffer's assistant.* "And I was still into excitement in a big way back then," he said, his smile charmingly self-deprecating. "From there it was a natural progression to stunt coordinator. And from there to directing heavy action movies."

"With a short stint directing an Oscar-caliber documentary tucked in there somewhere, too," Claire reminded him.

Rafe acknowledged her compliment with a nod. "So there you have it." He looked at her over the top of his beer as he lifted it to his lips. "The story of my life." He put the empty bottle down. "Now it's your turn."

"My turn?"

"The story of your life." He fastened his coffee-colored gaze on her face. "How'd you get to be the Claire Kingston sitting across from me right now?"

"Heavens," Claire said, flustered by his scrutiny. She didn't like to talk about herself or her life. "All you have to do is read the back issues of just about any tabloid or celebrity magazine. Every significant event of my life has been duly recorded for posterity."

"Surely not *every* event," he said, still staring at her intently.

"Every event that matters," she insisted. She held up one hand, fingers spread wide. "I was born—quite appropriately, according to the tabloids," she began humorously, ticking off the first significant event in her life on her little finger, "—on what would have been my parents' eleventh wedding anniversary if they hadn't gotten divorced and remarried in the interim. Although I don't remember it, I'm told that I spent my first birthday with my nanny in Beverly Hills while Mom and Dad were getting their second divorce in Mexico. Nothing much happened after that until I was four, then I made my acting debut in a bit part playing an angelic-looking, foulmouthed orphan opposite my father's then-current mistress, who was playing a nun. I smoked my first—and, thank God, only—cigarette in front of the camera when I was ten and promptly threw up all over Walter Matthau's shoes. I got my first kiss in *Age of Consent* when I was thirteen and won an Oscar for it." She ticked off all the fingers on one hand and, reversing their positions, began counting on the fingers of the other. "I did my first love scene when I was sixteen and then wasn't allowed to see the movie when it came out because it was R-rated," she continued, her tone less lighthearted than when she began her litany. "I also wore my first formal dress in that movie, in a scene where my character attends the junior prom."

Which had been the only junior prom she'd ever attended.

"Two years after that I starred in my first truly adult role in *The Deceivers*, I quit acting and—" she ticked off the tenth and final finger "—became the woman sitting here now." She turned her hands upright in a presenting gesture. "Claire Kingston, producer."

"Was it really your first kiss?"

"Yes," she said seriously. "It really was."

It had really been her first swearword, too. And her first cigarette. Her first formal dress. Her first love affair. And every single one of those firsts had happened on a movie set, in front of a dozen people. Every significant milestone in her life had been a pretense, the emotions of the moment manufactured for the camera. It had gotten so she'd begun to wonder whether she was capable of any real emotion, or if she'd even recognize one if she did experience it.

Which, she'd always felt, had led her directly to what had happened later.

"You finished here, folks?" the waitress asked, interrupting before Rafe could ask any more questions.

Claire looked up at her gratefully. "Yes, thank you. I am."

"Any dessert? Coffee?"

"No, not for me," Claire said. "Rafe?"

Rafe shook his head. "Just the check, please."

THEY EXITED the restaurant in silence, stepping out into the soft warmth of a Texas evening. The night air smelled of dust and sagebrush and the faint diesel fumes of the eighteen-wheelers that rolled down the highway separating the restaurant parking lot from that of the motel across the two-lane road. Traffic was light but Rafe took her hand as they crossed, as if she needed to be led to the safety of the other side.

Claire let him twine his fingers through hers without a murmur of protest. Without even a twinge of uneasiness, really. It felt right, having her hand in his. Warm and strong. And safe.

She looked up at him out of the corner of her eye as they strolled hand in hand past the motel office and the fenced-in swimming pool and the parked cars toward their rooms, wondering what it would be like with him.

Would he make love tenderly, the way he had kissed her last night? Or would he turn forceful and demanding? Would he wait for her to respond? Or rush her along before she was ready? Would he stop if she turned chicken and said no?

He was a big man. Strong and powerful. But he was also a gentleman. And a gentle man. He wouldn't hurt her, no matter what happened or how badly she behaved. And she *was* attracted to him, in spite of herself. She might never have a better opportunity to put her fears to rest.

Still, a knot of apprehension began coiling in her stomach as he let go of her hand to fish the room keys out of the front pocket of his tight-fitting black jeans.

Did she have the courage to seek out the answers to her questions? Or was she going to spend the rest of her life as an emotional cripple because she was too afraid to take a chance?

He pushed her door open. "Good night, Claire," he said softly. He picked up her hand, holding it palm up in his, and pressed her key into it. "Sleep tight." He started to turn toward his own room.

"Rafe?" she said, before she could stop herself.

He paused. "Yes?"

She swallowed to ease the dryness in her throat. She could feel the key biting into the soft flesh of her palm, spurring her on. "Kiss me good-night?" she whispered.

7

HER SOFTLY SPOKEN words slammed into Rafe like a fist to the solar plexus. He went perfectly still, struggling to absorb their exact meaning.

"Kiss me good-night?"

Her words undoubtedly meant just exactly what they implied. She wanted a good-night kiss from him. No more. No less.

Didn't she?

He turned back to face her fully, determined to give her exactly what she'd asked for and then let her take it from there. *No pressure,* he reminded himself. *No demands. Let her set the pace and lead the way.* He could do that, he told himself. He *had* to do that. He took a step closer to her and bent his head, just as he had the night before, keeping his hands at his sides and touching her with nothing but his mouth.

She was trembling. Violently.

He raised his head. "Claire?"

"Kiss me," she demanded in an anguished whisper. Her clenched fists came up against his chest as she leaned into him. "Please. Just kiss me."

He slid his arms around her and took her mouth with his.

She responded wildly, throwing her arms around his neck, lifting up on tiptoe to press her lips against his like a woman overcome with unrestrained, uncontrollable passion. He yielded to it for a moment, his arms pulling her tighter, his mouth opening wider, his tongue seeking, allowing himself to be swept up in the unexpected delight of her sensual demand. And then he realized that it wasn't passion that drove her but a sort of reckless, desperate bravado, like that of a terrified little girl throwing open the closet door to confront the monsters within.

Her body was taut and stiff in his arms, rather than pliant with need and heat. And the little sounds she was making in her throat weren't whimpers of passion but of fear.

His own ardor cooled instantly, as if someone had upended a bucket of ice water over him.

He slid his hands up her back to her head, cupping it, his fingers sliding into the strands of the French braid she'd woven it into after her shower. He pulled her head a little away from his, stopping the fevered assault on his mouth.

"Claire," he said, his breath warm against her lips. He could feel hers, fast and hard against his mouth, as if she'd been running a long way. He could feel her pulse, too, pounding against his thumbs where they touched her temples, and against the tips of his little fingers where they rested just under her jaw as he tilted her head back. "Claire. Take it easy, baby. Slow down.

This isn't a race. It's a kiss." He touched his lips to one corner of her mouth, and then the other. "Just a kiss."

She gave a long, shuddering gasp, like a child at the end of a crying jag, and went still in his arms, waiting.

"That's it," he murmured approvingly. He began nuzzling her, pressing soft, baby kisses to her cheeks and jaw and the closed lids of her eyes, gentling her, soothing her, calming her, until she relaxed against him. "That's it," he crooned, and brushed his lips over her mouth again.

She responded more naturally this time. A bit hesitantly but willingly. Her lips parted, giving him access. He took it, delicately, cautiously, sliding his tongue over her lips, flicking the tip between them, until she met it with her own. He explored her mouth, then, an invited guest rather than a conqueror, and she made him welcome with a soft, breathy sigh.

Claire floated on the feeling he engendered in her. He was warmth. And safety. And a subtle, half-realized excitement plucking at the edges of her consciousness. She felt as if she could go on kissing him like this forever, with his hands holding her head and his tongue filling her mouth.

There was nothing scary about kissing Rafe, she realized. Nothing dangerous. Nothing painful. It was an amazing discovery for a twenty-five-year-old woman to make. She found herself reveling in it. Relishing it. Wanting more.

Rafe felt the change in her immediately, felt the softening and the receptiveness. He shifted his hold on her, sliding his hands down the length of her spine, holding her to him as he took a step back to lean against the doorjamb, half in, half out of the open door of her motel room. The position brought her to rest between his thighs, pressing her breasts against his chest and giving his hands more freedom to roam the length of her body. He kept them above her tempting little bottom, contenting himself with running them up and down her back, occasionally letting his palms and fingertips glide down over the outside curve of her hips.

She'd changed clothes after her shower, trading her prissy, touch-me-not, lady-executive suit for a pair of soft khaki chinos and an even softer silk shirt. The fabric slid against her back under his caressing hands, warming and exciting them both. He could feel the narrow band of her bra under his palms. It was driving him crazy, tempting him to follow it around to the front of her body and fill his hands with her sweet little breasts.

But he didn't think she was ready for that.

Was she?

She was pressed against him, warm and willing. One hand was in his hair, stroking it, over and over, as they kissed. Her mouth was moist and giving, open under his.

Maybe she *was* ready for the next step.

He slid his hands around to her sides, under her upraised arms, and pressed his palms lightly against the sides of her breasts.

She stiffened.

He took his hands away.

"No," she murmured against his mouth. "It's all right. You just startled me." Her voice shook a little. "It's really all right."

But he knew it wasn't.

The soft receptiveness had gone out of her, replaced by renewed traces of fear. And he didn't want even a trace of fear coloring her response to him. Not a hint to mar the experience for either of them. When she finally gave herself to him, it would be totally, without reservation.

"We've got another long day ahead of us tomorrow, honey," he murmured softly as he loosened his hold on her.

She remained very still, leaning against him as if she were afraid to move. "But you're . . . that is, you've got a . . ." she said, confused by the dichotomy between his physical and verbal responses.

"Got a hard-on?" he said bluntly, knowing that was what she was referring to. "Yeah, I do." He linked his hands at the small of her back and rested his forehead against hers. "But didn't anybody ever tell you that a guy doesn't have to score a home run every time he's up at bat?"

She pulled back a little to look up at him. "He doesn't?" she asked with obvious skepticism.

He wondered whether it was the information itself that was news to her or the fact a man was the one advocating restraint. "No, he doesn't." He unlinked his hands and set them on the curve of her waist. "I thought that was something every girl learned by the time she was in high school. At least—" he cocked an eyebrow at her "—every girl who had older brothers to look out for her."

"I didn't go to high school," Claire said. "I had a tutor on the set. And Gage and Pierce were both adults with their own lives by the time I was a teenager," she added, in automatic defense of her brothers.

"Well, then, let me clue you in to a few things that seem to have been left out of your education, Ms. Kingston. Unfulfilled desire can be frustrating as hell for a man—or a woman, for that matter—but it isn't fatal." *Even when you might wish it was!* "And a hard-on isn't something a woman has to do anything about unless she wants to. Is that clear?" He lifted a hand to her chin, tilting it up to make her look at him. "Clear?" he demanded.

"Yes," Claire said faintly, not knowing whether to be embarrassed or relieved. She decided she was both. "Clear."

"Good. Make sure you remember it." He kissed her once more, softly but lingeringly so that they were both breathing a little heavier when he finally raised his head. "Good night, Claire," he murmured huskily, and resolutely set her away from him.

She stood there, a little dazed, and stared up at him.

"Go on." He gave her a gentle nudge, urging her to step back across the threshold into her motel room as he moved away from it. "I'll wait right here until I hear you lock your door."

"Good night, Rafe." She looked up at him with something like wonder in her eyes. "And thank you," she whispered, just before she closed the door.

Rafe waited until he heard the dead bolt click into place, and then he turned away from her door and walked the few feet separating it from his own. He couldn't make the key fit into the lock on the first try, and had to stop and swear and steady himself before he tried it again.

"I hope to God they have cable TV here," he mumbled when he finally got the door open. There was no way he was getting any sleep tonight. Not with every male hormone in his body screaming for release into the soft, sweet body of the woman in the next room.

THE NEXT MORNING could have been awkward—*should* have been awkward, Claire thought—but it wasn't. Because Rafe wouldn't let it be. They had breakfast together in the deceptive cool of the early morning and then stopped at a convenience store to get a cooler and stock it with fruit, snacks and soft drinks. Rafe teased her about the granola bars and "designer water" she selected and she twitted him about the Doritos, M&M's and Dr Pepper he seemed to deem essential to highway travel. Their rented Blazer was gassed up and on the road by eight-thirty, its boxy hood pointed toward the western horizon and the morning sun shining in through the back window.

Claire couldn't remember a time she'd ever felt more relaxed and carefree.

Part of it was just being away from Hollywood. Away from the backbiting and the back stabbing. Away from the tabloids and the gossip, the multimillion-dollar deals that hinged on somebody's ego, and the endless lunches where reputations were made and lost over poached salmon and arugula with warm goat cheese and sun-dried tomatoes.

Part of it was just the simple pleasure of being out on the road on a beautiful day, driving down an endless ribbon of highway with the windows open and the radio on and nothing but possibilities ahead.

But another part of it—the biggest part of it—was less than three feet away from her. She looked over at him, sitting there behind the wheel, his eyes focused on the road ahead, his big body relaxed, rock solid and utterly reliable.

His profile was severe and uncompromising—a broad, smooth forehead, sharp blade of a nose, chiseled cheekbones, commanding chin—softened only by the curve of his clean-cut lips, the sweep of his lashes and the ebony waves of his thick hair, blowing in the warm wind coming in through the open window. His hands on the wheel were strong and sure, his palms firm against the molded plastic, his fingers lightly tapping out a rhythm in time with the country song on the radio. His shoulders were broad and rounded with muscle under the soft fabric of his western-cut shirt. His torso was wedge shaped, his belly hard and flat beneath his silver concha belt buckle. His athlete's thighs strained against the faded black denim of his jeans.

He exuded strength and sexuality and confidence. He promised tenderness. He inspired trust.

Claire felt that cold, hidden little place inside her, the one she'd been carrying around for so long, begin to melt a few critical degrees as she stared at him.

"What?" he asked, feeling her gaze on him like a caress. "Do I have gravy on my chin?" He'd had sausage, biscuits and country gravy for breakfast, another Southern dietary oddity she'd teased him about as she ate her bran flakes with skim milk.

Claire shook her head. "I was just wondering how soon we'd get to Flat Rock."

He gave her a wary look out of the corner of his eye. "Are you in some kind of hurry?"

"No." But she was. Her curiosity about him was rapidly turning from merely intense to insatiable. "I just like to be able to plan things, is all."

"No?" Rafe feigned exaggerated astonishment. "Really?"

He was rewarded by her soft laugh.

"I told my mother not to expect us until sometime after three," he informed her.

"I thought Flat Rock was less than fifty miles away."

"As the crow flies," he agreed. "But we aren't flying. Or even taking a semidirect route. There are a lot of small towns down the side roads between Ropesville and Flat Rock. Maybe one of them will be Burley."

"Maybe," was all she would say.

They arrived in Flat Rock earlier than he'd estimated, because Claire had only needed a minute or two to decide that none of the towns they'd passed through on their circuitous way to his hometown were what she was looking for. By the time they drove past the official "Entering Flat Rock, pop. 973" sign at the edge of town, Rafe had developed a healthy appreciation for what the location manager must have been going through for the past month.

Nothing they saw met her exacting standards.

"The high school is too modern," she'd said of one town.

"Too many billboards on the main street," she'd said of another.

"Not 'country' enough."

"There should be an old-fashioned bandstand on the square."

"The courthouse should be brick, not fieldstone."

"No soda shop."

"Too run-down."

"Too new."

"The office park ruins it."

Rafe finally quit pointing out that merchants could be paid to take down billboards, that grips could build the required bandstand or construct a temporary brick facade for the courthouse, that they weren't going to shoot any scenes using an office park so it didn't matter whether there was one or not. Claire refused to listen.

"Just what the hell are you looking for?" he demanded at one point.

"Burley," she replied coolly. Unimpressed and un-intimidated by his glower, she turned her attention back to her map and made a little red *X*, indicating that an-other town had been vetoed.

Rafe struggled to hide an admiring grin. She might be uncertain about some things, but her career wasn't one of them. She approached the hunt for the fictional Burley like a field general on reconnaissance, and she wasn't about to settle for anything less than exactly what she wanted.

Which was what made his grin fade as they turned off Farm Road 179 onto the main street of Flat Rock. She lowered her map, looking around her with a specula-tive gleam in her big blue eyes.

Flat Rock was a real old-fashioned country town. It was a little worn around the edges, a little weathered, but well cared for by its proud, upstanding citizens. The high school was twenty-five years old, with wooden bleachers on either side of the football field and an old-fashioned, nonelectronic scoreboard. There was a wooden bandstand on the square. And a soda foun-tain visible through the plate glass window of the local drugstore.

"The courthouse isn't brick," Rafe said, feeling compelled to point that out before she got any bright ideas.

"But the bank is," Claire noted, studying the stately old building as they drove past. "I'm sure something could be worked out with the owners if we wanted to use it."

"The city fathers were building an office park at the other end of town last time I was here." He speeded up a little so they would get to it sooner. "A big one. Very modern. With a really fake-looking pseudowestern facade."

Claire stopped twisting around in her seat, trying to take it all in at once, and turned to face him. "You knew Flat Rock would make the perfect Burley all along," she accused. "Probably as soon as you read the screenplay. Why didn't you say something? It would have saved everybody a lot of wasted time and effort."

"Flat Rock? As Burley?" he scoffed. "You've got to be kidding."

"I'm not kidding and you know it. It's perfect. The town square. The bandstand. The high school. The— Oh, my God. Is that the library?" Some of the most important scenes in the movie would take place in a library. "It's *perfect!* Pull over and stop," she ordered eagerly. "I want to look at the inside."

THEY WERE STILL discussing the suitability of using Flat Rock for the fictional Burley when Rafe turned into the parking lot of the Motel 6 located on the outskirts of town, where the state highway and the farm road that led to Flat Rock's main street intersected.

"I can't believe you don't see it," Claire said, shaking her head as she got out of the Blazer. "It's exactly—*exactly* right." She closed the car door. "Maybe you're just too close to it," she suggested, searching for a reason to explain his appalling lapse in artistic vision.

"Maybe," Rafe said morosely. *And maybe I just don't want the damned movie made here,* he added silently.

He'd spent a good portion of the past fifteen years of his life trying to shake the dust of Flat Rock off his boots, to get away from its small-minded, tradition-bound, provincial citizens. Oh, he'd been back now and again. For his sisters' weddings, the high school graduation of each of his siblings, the occasional christening of a new niece or nephew when he could. But never for more than a day or two at a time. And there was no way in hell he wanted to spend any longer than that in Flat Rock now, shooting a movie that would require him to be there for forty-eight consecutive days.

He felt stifled in Flat Rock. Hemmed in by the expectations and preconceptions of the townspeople. Judged. Here, he would always be that poor kid from the wrong side of the tracks, that hot-eyed young Mexican boy who'd gotten above himself when he came sniffing around Laura Lyn Parker and then gotten exactly what he deserved when she dumped him.

Surely, he thought, in all of the great state of Texas, there was some place other than Flat Rock that Claire would be willing to use as the backdrop for *Desperado.*

"I'm going to call Tony as soon as we get checked in," she said excitedly. Tony was the location manager, the man responsible for seeing that the shoot ran smoothly, from feeding the cast and crew while they were on location to arranging things over at city hall when they wanted to block traffic for filming. "He'll need to get out tomorrow and get busy with his end of it if we're going to start shooting on schedule. There's barely enough time to get everything done as it is. I need to call Robert," she said, half to herself, "so he can let everyone else know what's going on. Dennis and Becky and R.J. are going to need to fly out here ASAP, too, and get cracking on their end of things."

"You're just going to go ahead with this? Without my agreement?"

She looked at him over the hood of the car. "Why, in heaven's name, *wouldn't* you agree?" she asked reasonably, ready to listen if he had any legitimate concerns. As the director, he was the one who had to visualize and set up the scenes to be shot. His cooperation was essential. "It's not as if we have a lot of time to find someplace else, and Flat Rock *is* perfect. Unless there's something I don't know that would make it unsuitable? Are the bureaucrats down at city hall likely to give us a hard time or something?"

He shook his head. The bureaucrats at city hall were likely to give her the keys to the city once they found out she wanted to shoot a movie in their town. They were likely to erect a statue in her honor when they realized how much money was going to come flooding into the local economy as a result.

"Then what?" Claire said, honestly puzzled by his reluctance.

But pride wouldn't let him tell her. Pride, and the sneaking suspicion that his objections amounted to little more than the leftover insecurities of a boy. He hated a whiner. And that's what he would be if he voiced the nebulous reasons for his dissension.

"Nothing," he said. "You're absolutely right. Flat Rock is perfect."

8

THERE WERE ALREADY four cars parked in front of his mother's house when they arrived. Rafe recognized all of them. The dusty 4 × 4 ranch pickup with the gun rack across the back window that belonged to his sister, Inez's, rancher husband; the lovingly maintained, souped-up Trans Am Mercedes's Jimmy Lee still hot-rodded around in, despite the pair of toddler-size car seats in the back; the rattletrap old Mustang his brother, Luis, insisted on calling a classic; and the silver Taurus he'd bought for his mother a few years ago, fancied up with a Texas Tech sticker in the back window, a toy oil derrick with a tiny Texas flag on top fastened to the dashboard and a miniature Piper Cherokee hanging from the rearview mirror. The only one missing was Ramona's flashy little red Miata, but since she lived a good fifteen-hour drive away in Dallas he wasn't surprised.

Rafe couldn't suppress a grin as he surveyed the motley collection of vehicles. Texans did love their cars. Even sweet little Texas matrons like his mother. It made him wish he'd driven his old bathtub Porsche out from California. It would have given the family—especially Jimmy Lee—a real thrill.

"Looks like everybody's already here," he said to Claire as he shouldered open the door of the rented Blazer.

"Are you sure this outfit is all right?" she asked, gesturing down at her clothes as she got out on her side without waiting for him to come around and open the door for her. "Maybe I should have worn something a little dressier."

"Like one of those suits of yours?" Rafe shook his head. "Trust me, you look fine."

She was wearing a pale blue silk camp shirt tucked neatly into the waistband of a fresh pair of khaki chino slacks. Her thick sable hair was woven into another one of those complicated-looking braids at the back of her head, and she wore a pair of flat, strappy sandals on her feet. He was sure she thought the outfit was appropriately conservative and suitable for a lady executive at leisure. And it was. It also showed off her innate sense of style and showcased her slender cover-girl figure to perfection: the silk of her blouse clinging softly to her small, sweet breasts; the expensive woven leather belt emphasizing the narrowness of her waist; the tailored slacks outlining the gentle flare of her hips. Her Italian leather sandals exposed toenails painted a bright, unexpected red.

Rafe let his gaze move slowly up and down her body as he came around the hood of the car. "More than fine," he said, giving her a playfully lascivious grin.

Claire's cheeks warmed in pleasure and confusion. She looked away. "Maybe I should wear the jacket," she murmured, leaning back inside the open car door to rescue the cream-colored linen blazer he thought he'd convinced her she'd be more comfortable without.

He took her hand. "Leave it," he said, pulling her back before she could get the jacket. He pushed the door closed with a thud. "Come on." He tucked her hand into the crook of his elbow. "I'll teach you how to mingle just for fun."

He bypassed the path to the front door of the little whitewashed clapboard house, following a more traveled one around the side that wound between the overgrown pink crepe myrtle bushes and the detached garage his mother used for storage rather than the purpose for which it was intended. The smell of burning mesquite and grilling meat filled the air, mixing with the heat of the late afternoon and the sweet scent of summer flowers. The sound of voices, a drawling Texas twang mixed with the sibilant, musical cadence of Spanish, rose louder as they approached the back of the house. They could hear the clicking whir of an automatic sprinkler and the shrill laughter of excited children.

"Sounds like the rug rats are having fun," Rafe said. A particularly high-pitched shriek rent the air, followed by a threat to mash someone's face in. "Especially Susana," he added, recognizing the voice of his ten-year-old niece. He looked down at the woman beside him. "Are you sure you want to go to this shindig? You could be taking your life in your— Uh-oh, too late. We've been spotted." He released her hand and held out his arms to the small, smiling woman who came hurrying toward them across the backyard. "Mama," he said, catching her up against him.

Claire understood only one word—*Rafael*—in the torrent of Spanish that followed, but she recognized a loving scold when she heard it. Rafe answered his mother in the same language, laughing and shaking his head at whatever she'd said before he turned to introduce Claire.

Claire didn't know quite what she had expected the widowed, hardworking mother of seven grown children to look like, but it certainly wasn't the trim little woman standing in front of her now. In place of a stoop-shouldered, careworn figure dressed in unrelieved black was a sprightly woman wearing a red bandanna-print cotton shirtwaist dress and canvas espadrilles. Her short dark hair was liberally laced with gray, and her eyes were the same penetrating, hot-coffee brown as her son's.

"Mama, this is Claire Kingston," Rafe said. "Claire, my mother, Dolores Santana."

Claire took the strong, work-hardened hand the other woman held out to her. "I'm very pleased to meet you, Mrs. Santana," she said, mentally chiding herself for the sin of thinking in clichés. "Rafe has told me a lot about you."

Dolores cast a speculative look up at her tall son. "Has he now?" she said in a tone that had Rafe mentally squirming. She turned her attention back to Claire. "He hasn't told us a thing about you. Come."

She patted the smooth, slender hand she still held in hers. "Come and meet my daughters," she said, "and tell us all about this movie you're making with Rafael."

"Mama," Rafe tried, knowing it was useless. "I really don't think Claire wants to talk business. This is supposed to be a party."

"Oh, I don't mind," Claire said, just as he had known she would.

"See? She doesn't mind." Dolores waved her free hand at her son. "Go away, Rafael, and talk to your brothers. Luis has been waiting to show you what he and Jimmy Lee have done to his car. And I am sure Miguel—" Miguel was Inez's husband "—needs some help with the barbecue. I will bring her back to you later. After we have become acquainted."

"But—" Rafe searched for a reason to keep Claire out of his mother's clutches "—she hasn't met everyone yet."

"There's no need to overwhelm her with everyone all at once," Dolores said serenely. "Better if she meets us one at a time."

"Well, *I* haven't said hello to everyone yet, either."

"You can say hello to your sisters later, when it is time to eat." She drew Claire away with her, leaving Rafe staring after them.

"HERE YA GO, buddy." His brother-in-law, Jimmy Lee, pressed a cold beer into his hand.

"Thanks," Rafe mumbled. He lifted the bottle to his lips and took a long swallow, his eyes on Claire and his mother as they headed toward the group of women clustered around the picnic table under a large cottonwood tree.

"She corralled Luis's date, too." Jimmy Lee nodded toward the pretty blond sitting at one end of the picnic table. A bright-eyed toddler—one of Jimmy Lee and Mercedes's twins—was perched in her lap.

Luis glowered darkly. "Mama's had her over there for the last thirty minutes, gabbing like a magpie."

"She's been pumpin' her for information," Miguel said, looking up from the grill to add his two cents to the conversation. "Tryin' to find out just how much carryin' on the two of you are doing up there at Tech while you're out of her sight." He cast a sly look at Rafe. "Just like she's gonna do with Rafe's little lady friend."

Rafe grunted and took another swallow of beer. "Doesn't Mama know this is the nineties? Men and women don't congregate on opposite sides of the room at parties anymore."

"They do in Flat Rock," Rafe's youngest brother, Matteo, said as he handed a bowl of spicy barbecue sauce to the chef. "Especially when Mama's after information."

The men shared a brief, commiserating silence as Miguel slathered barbecue sauce over the ribs and chicken on the grill.

"That isn't going to be ready for another hour, at least," Jimmy Lee said when Miguel was finished basting the meat. "Come on." He gestured with his beer. "Let's go out front and I'll show you what I did to Luis's Mustang."

"HOW LONG HAVE YOU and Rafael been seeing each other?" Dolores asked, wasting no time on subtleties.

"Seeing each other?" Claire said, surprised at the question. She'd been expecting to be asked about the movie business. "Rafe and I aren't 'seeing each other.' We just work together. We're, ah..." What did you call a man you weren't 'seeing' but who had kissed you silly just the night before? "Colleagues," she decided, hoping the warmth in her face would be attributed to the heat. "Business colleagues."

Dolores Santana looked unconvinced. "Rafael has never brought a business colleague home to meet his family before."

"Oh, well, ah . . ." Claire didn't know what to say to that. "He didn't bring me here to meet his family, exactly. It's just that we were in the area, scouting locations for *Desperado* and—" she shrugged "—here we are."

"Desperado? Scouting locations? What does this mean?"

"For heaven's sake, Mama," said one of the other women before Claire could answer, "at least let her sit down before you start with the third degree."

She smiled at Claire and scooted over, patting the wooden seat beside her. "I'm Inez, Rafe's oldest sister," she said as Claire sat down. "And that's Mercedes." She gestured toward the heavily pregnant woman sitting near the head of the table in an upholstered armchair. "And Sandy, a friend of Luis's from Tech. That's one of Mercedes's twins, Dorrie, on her lap." She put her arm around the shoulders of the young girl who'd come up to lean against her while she was making the introductions. "And Susana, my oldest."

"Would you like something to drink?" Mercedes asked, taking over the duties of hostess when Inez bent her head to listen to whatever her daughter wanted to whisper in her ear. "Beer?" She put her hands on the arms of her chair, preparing to push herself up. "Lemonade?"

"No, please don't get up," Claire said. "If you'll just tell me where the lemonade is—"

"Oh, don't worry, I'm not nearly as far along as I look," Mercedes said, waving away Claire's obvious concern. "And the exercise is good for me. Mama?" she asked as she filled a plastic glass with lemonade from the five-gallon thermos on the end of the table. "Would you like another one while I'm up?"

Dolores shook her head impatiently.

"You'll have to ask your daddy when it's going to be ready," Claire heard Inez say to her daughter. "He's in charge of the barbecue."

The little girl scurried off toward the front of the house.

"When are you due?" Claire asked curiously, eying Mercedes's huge belly as she accepted the glass of lemonade. Tara hadn't been that big on the day she delivered.

"Not for three-and-a-half months yet. But it's another set of twins, so it looks as if I'm going to pop any minute." She bent her knees a bit, feeling behind her for the arms of the chair with her hands. "Jimmy Lee thinks it's wonderful, of course," she said as she lowered herself into the seat. "He's *real* proud of himself for hittin' doubles again." She rolled her eyes expressively. "He even thinks we ought to try for two more in another couple of years." Her smile was pure feminine devilishness. "But I told him I'd cut it off for him myself if he tries to come near me again without gettin' clipped first. I love my babies dearly but these two—" she patted her distended stomach fondly "—are going to be the last."

Dolores Santana waited until the feminine laughter had died down to resume her interrogation. "So...how long have you and Rafael been business colleagues?" she asked Claire, taking up right where she had left off.

"Mama!" Inez and Mercedes voiced their protests at the same time, in exactly the same tone of exasperation.

"What?" Dolores flashed her two daughters a quelling look. "I shouldn't be interested in my oldest son's job?" She waved her hands at them. "Tell me," she demanded as she turned back to Claire.

RAFE WONDERED what Claire was thinking, sitting there on the other side of the food-laden picnic table between Jimmy Lee and Matteo. He wondered what she thought of his family and if she was comparing this party to the one at her brother's Beverly Hills mansion. Not, he thought, that there *was* any comparison between champagne in crystal glasses and cold Lone Star straight out of the bottle; between exotic food served on fine china and a backyard barbecue dished up on paper plates; between live music provided by a professional Hollywood orchestra and country tunes coming from a tape player; between his homespun, down-home family and the glittering superstars of Hollywood.

She didn't look as if she were making comparisons, he thought, but then, considering who she was and where she'd come from, how could she not? Especially when he couldn't keep from making them himself.

"What exactly does a producer do?" asked Matteo after the first few minutes of silent, concentrated eating were over and everyone was ready to focus on something other than food.

"Well," Claire wiped her mouth with a paper napkin, "a producer sort of…oversees things, I guess is the best way to put it. Once a decision has been made to do a certain project, the producer starts putting together the creative team. Writer, director, set decorators, cinematographer—that's a cameraman—" she explained, "and all the rest of the cast and crew. The producer's also responsible for setting the budget and schedules, and seeing that they're adhered to. Of course—" she flashed a quick look across the table at Rafe to see if he was listening "—the producer works very closely with the director on all of this. His input is very important to the success of a movie and a good producer always considers her director's wishes."

"Unless they conflict with hers," Rafe said dryly.

THE SUN HUNG LOW in the western sky, just beginning to paint the horizon with faint watercolor traces of pink and orange. The kids had settled down, the three oldest ones feeding apples through the fence to a neighbor's goats, the younger ones bedded down inside. Mercedes was snoozing in her upholstered armchair. Miguel was cleaning the grill. Jimmy Lee was out front, fooling around under the hood of somebody's car with Matteo. Inez and Dolores were in the kitchen, seeing about coffee and dessert. Luis and the pretty blond co-ed who'd come down with him from Texas Tech were leaning on the fence that separated the backyard from the open pasture beyond, exchanging giggles and sweet talk.

Rafe watched Claire as she sat alone at the picnic table, her chin propped up on the backs of her entwined fingers, staring at the deepening colors of the sunset.

She'd fit in with his family better than he had expected, showing little of her usual aloofness toward people she didn't know well. Not, Rafe thought with a smile, that anyone could remain aloof for long with a bunch of forward, talkative Texans pelting you with nosy questions from all sides. She'd borne the interrogation with fortitude and style, even going so far as to promise to see what she could do about getting Matteo a personally autographed poster of Heather Locklear wearing as little as possible.

Taking the first opportunity to be alone with her since they'd arrived at his mother's, Rafe ambled over to where she was sitting and eased his big frame down beside her onto the wooden bench seat. Leaning his elbows back on the checkered tablecloth, he stretched his jeans-clad legs out in front of him and crossed his booted ankles. "Tired?"

Claire turned her head, her chin still resting on her hands, and gave him a soft smile. "A little, I guess. But it's a nice tired." She gave a little sigh of contentment and turned her gaze back to the horizon. "It's beautiful, isn't it?"

"Sure is," Rafe said, staring at her profile.

"We don't get sunsets like this in L.A.," she commented. "Those colors are incredible. So vivid and intense. We're going to have to make sure to take advantage of them in one or two scenes in *Desperado*."

"Is that all a beautiful sunset makes you think of?" Rafe said, amused. "How you can make use of it in a movie?"

"Well, no." She lowered her hands, still clasped, to the table. "But I was just sitting here, thinking—"

"About the movie," Rafe snorted in good-natured disgust.

"Among other things."

"What other things?" Rafe demanded teasingly. "I dare you to name one."

"Just...other things," Claire said, trying for her usual cool. And failing. Miserably. She'd been thinking about him. And about the way he'd kissed her last night. And wondering if he was going to kiss her tonight.

And what she would do when he did.

"Why, Claire Kingston—" he raised his hand, his elbow still on the table, and rubbed the back of one finger lightly against her cheek "—is that a blush I see?"

She clasped her hands tighter together as the warmth of his touch zinged through her. "Merely a reflection of the sunset," she said primly.

And Rafe laughed knowingly and lowered his hand.

"Coffee and dessert in the kitchen," Inez shouted from the back door, letting the screen slam behind her as she went back inside. Three small bodies streaked by the picnic table in answer to their mother's call. Mercedes roused from her light doze in the chair and pushed herself to her feet. Miguel put the lid on the grill and turned toward the house.

"Feel up to dessert?" Rafe asked as Luis and Sandy strolled by the table, hand in hand, on their way to the kitchen.

Claire slanted him a disbelieving look out of the corner of her eyes. "After that dinner I ate?"

She'd had macaroni salad, baked beans, coleslaw, homegrown tomato relish, cucumber pickles, molded raspberry Jell-O with fruit cocktail and a deviled egg. An extra plate had been provided to hold two ears of roasted corn, dripping with butter, and a baked potato wrapped in foil. She'd eaten everything except one ear of corn and half of the potato.

"I made a complete and utter pig of myself," she groaned.

Rafe might have agreed with her if he hadn't seen the moderate portions she'd had to begin with. One of Mercedes's two-year-old twins could eat more than she had. "It's strawberry shortcake," he said.

Claire shook her head. "I'm so full, I can't even be tempted."

Rafe grinned, recognizing a challenge when he heard one, even if she didn't realize one had been issued. He leaned closer so he could whisper in her ear. "Homemade strawberry shortcake," he murmured, using the same voice he'd use when offering other, more earthy temptations. "With homemade buttermilk shortcake. And fresh-off-the-vine strawberries from Inez's strawberry patch. And real, honest-to-goodness cream, whipped up soft—" he drew the words out slowly, seductively "—and sweet with a little vanilla and sugar."

Claire felt her heartbeat begin to quicken with what she realized was anticipation. And it wasn't for strawberry shortcake!

"Are you sure I can't tempt you to try it?" he crooned in her ear. "Just a bite?"

When he used that voice, she thought, rising to follow him into the house, he could probably tempt her to try anything.

"OH, RAFE LIKES to think of himself as one tough hombre," Inez said with a soft laugh. She put another saucer on the drain board for Claire to dry. "And, I'll admit, he's got a hide like one of Miguel's prize bulls. And a head like one, too, once he gets an idea in it," she added. "But he's got a heart made of pure marshmallow fluff. Remember the strays he was always bringing home with him, Mama?" she asked, glancing over to where her mother was wrapping up leftovers for her brood to take home with them. "Injured birds. Possums. Rabbits," she said, turning back to Claire. "He even brought an armadillo home once. The poor ugly little thing had barely escaped being road kill out on the highway and Rafe just had to nurse it back to health."

"I had to nurse what back to health?" Rafe demanded, coming into the kitchen in time to hear his name mentioned. He'd been searching for Claire, wondering if she'd had enough yet and was ready to leave. It surprised him to find her in the kitchen, drying dishes. He wouldn't have thought she knew how.

"That half-dead armadillo you found on the highway," Inez said. "Remember? You brought it home and kept it in a wooden produce box until it was well enough to turn loose."

Rafe shook his head. "I never did anything like that. You must be thinking of Matteo."

"Well, Matteo, too, of course." The "of course" was because Matteo had plans to be a veterinarian. "But you did it, too." She glanced at her mother. "Didn't he, Mama?"

Dolores nodded.

"He tamed a half-wild kitten one time," Inez said to Claire. "Remember that, Rafe? It was a little calico. You should have seen him with it. This big scrawny fifteen-year-old kid, sweet-talking this little tiny cat. I'm telling you," she said, shaking her head, remembering, "it was a sight. Took him a couple of weeks to get it to let him pet it, but he never got impatient. Never tried to force it to come to him. Just kind of coaxed it along until, finally, it started following him around like a dog. I wonder whatever happened to that cat," she mused as she rinsed another saucer and set it on the counter.

Claire automatically picked it up and began drying it, but she wasn't really paying any attention to what she was doing. She was thinking of Rafe and his marshmallow heart and his injured birds and his wounded armadillo and his little half-wild cat, and wondering if she fit in there somewhere. Was she some kind of injured bird to him? Some kind of little wounded, half-wild animal that needed careful handling to be tamed?

It would be humiliating to think she was. To think that the only reason he had kissed her so tenderly and held her so gently was because he saw her as some kind of . . . of charity case that needed healing. And yet . . . maybe that was exactly what she needed. Someone who would treat her very gently and patiently.

" . . . lived to be almost sixteen years old," Dolores was saying. "I had Matteo bury it out around the side of the house, under the crepe myrtle bush where it liked to sleep in the afternoons."

"Why, you sentimental old thing, you," Inez teased. "I didn't know you had it in—"

"Jimmy Lee said he and Mercedes are gettin' ready to pack up the twins and call it a day," Luis announced, letting the screen door slam behind him as he entered the kitchen. "He says she's tired and he wants to get her home to bed. Sandy and Matteo and I are going over to Buck's—" Buck's was a honky-tonk out close to the main highway "—to listen to the new band they're tryin' out tonight." He looked at his brother. "You and Claire wanna come with us?"

"They've got live music at Buck's now?" In his day, Buck's had had a jukebox, a bar and a couple of pool tables in the back. It wasn't the kind of place he'd have taken a date.

"Dancin', too," Luis said.

"What kind of crowd?" Rafe wanted to know.

Luis managed to look offended. "It's an okay crowd," he said. "I wouldn't take Sandy to some kind of joint. You wanna come with us or not?"

"I don't know." Rafe looked at Claire. "You feel up to a little honky-tonkin' before we call it a night?" he asked, silently willing her to say yes. He'd like to hold her in his arms while they danced to cowboy ballads and country love songs, to feel her body move in rhythm with his. "We won't stay if you don't like it."

"I'd like to," she said. "It sounds like fun."

THE CROWD AT BUCK'S was predictably light on a weekday night. The four-piece band was fair-to-middlin' and not too loud, as was often the case in country bars. Rafe didn't even wait for the drinks to be delivered before he coaxed Claire to her feet and headed for the dance floor. "Come on," he said, taking her by the hand as the band struck up a slow country tune. "I'll teach you the two-step."

She went with him willingly, looking up at him with complete trust as he swung her into place in front of him.

"We do country dancing a bit differently than what you're used to. I put my hand here," he said, placing his right hand on her shoulder, close to the curve of her neck, "and you put yours—"

"Here." She placed her left hand on his side, just above the waistband of his jeans. "I saw *Urban Cowboy*," she told him with a saucy smile.

He smiled back. "Okay, the basic step is real easy. You just kind of slide your feet. Ready? Back, back, together. Back, back, together. That's it," he crooned approvingly as she followed his lead. "Soften your knees a little. Good. Now, relax your shoulders." He flexed his fingers against her shoulder and neck, squeezing the muscles until they loosened. "That's it." He smiled down at her as they moved around the minuscule dance floor. "You're doing the two-step. What do you think of it so far?"

She thought it was wonderful—so far. "It seems to me there was a little more to it in *Urban Cowboy*."

"Does that mean you're ready to try a few turns?"

If doing a few turns meant he had to hold her a little closer then, "Yes," she murmured, she was definitely ready to try a few turns.

He curled his hand more firmly around the back of her neck to guide her, automatically pulling her a little closer to his chest. She came closer than she had to. Not so close that they were actually touching but close enough so they could feel the heat of each other's bodies. Rafe held her carefully, maintaining the distance she had put between them as they made half-a-dozen gliding turns around the floor.

"I'm going to twirl you now," he murmured, warning her a second before his hand tightened on her neck to guide her into the maneuver. She twirled once slowly, passing under his upraised arm, turning on the ball of her foot until she had made a complete circle. They were only millimeters apart now. He took another gliding step and twirled her again, a bit faster, bringing her a bit closer. They were chest-to-breast when she faced him again, their bodies touching, their eyes locked, the air between them suddenly steamy with possibilities and need.

Rafe tightened his hand on the nape of her neck, tilting her head back so that the weight of it rested in his palm and her perfect cherry-red lips were only a breath beneath his, poised for the taking. Claire tightened her hand at his waist, curling her fingers into the fabric of his shirt, and held on for dear life. Their clasped hands were down at their sides, their fingers linked, palms pressed tightly together, forearms entwined.

She could feel every subtle movement in the muscles of his outer thigh with the back of her hand as he danced her around the floor. Every deep breath he took against the softness of her lips. Every labored beat of his heart against her breast. Every involuntary twitch of the rock-hard erection pressed against her stomach.

She tensed a bit, waiting for the fear to come. He loosened his hold immediately, before it could. She sighed and relaxed completely into his embrace, as trusting as a kitten in familiar hands. The slow country song segued into another ballad, equally slow, the singer crooning the words to an old Kenny Rogers tune about a cowboy's desperate longing for his lady.

Rafe brushed her lips with his and whispered her name.

"Yes." Claire sighed tremulously and closed her eyes.

"No," Rafe said. "Look at me."

Her lashes lifted slowly, as if the weight of them made it hard for her to open her eyes.

"I think I know what you want," Rafe rasped in that deep whiskey-through-gravel voice of his that sent fire licking along all her nerve endings, "what you're inviting me to do, but thinking isn't enough. You've got to tell me. Straight out. Claire?" His hot-coffee eyes bored into hers, fiery and intense. "You've got to tell me what you want before this goes any further."

She met his gaze unflinchingly, every growing desire, every lingering doubt, plain in the jeweled depths of her sapphire eyes.

She only wanted what other women wanted. Love. Passion. And the freedom and ability to express and experience both without fear. Something told her that Rafe Santana, with his hot eyes and gentle hands and even gentler kisses could give her those things. Or set her on the right path to finding them for herself. All she had to do was be brave enough to take the first step.

"Claire?"

"I want you to make love to me, Rafe," she whispered achingly. "Please."

9

RAFE COULD NEVER REMEMBER, later, what excuse he'd given to his brothers to explain why he and Claire had to leave Buck's in such a hurry. He barely remembered the four-mile drive from the roadside honky-tonk to the motel where they were staying. But he would remember forever the expression in her wide blue eyes as he closed the door to his motel room with both of them inside.

Passion. Uncertainty. Determination. Fear.

The way she stood there, staring at him, made him think of that little cat again and the way it had looked at him when it was trying to work up the courage to take that first bite of food from his hand. But Claire wasn't a cat. And her feelings and needs weren't that simple. And maybe, he thought, staring at the jumble of emotions in her eyes, maybe he was being a fool to think he could deal with them as if they were.

"Are you sure you want to do this, honey?" Rafe murmured.

Claire lifted her chin. "Yes, of course," she said with a brave attempt at recapturing some of her characteristic haughtiness. "I said I did, didn't I?"

Slowly, carefully, Rafe held out his hand. "Then come here."

She hovered uncertainly, eyeing him warily from halfway across the room. Her body was tense, quivering with nerves and conflicting impulses. Wanting. And so afraid of where that wanting would lead. She'd had time to reconsider her rash invitation between the dance floor and the bedroom. He could see her weighing her alternatives, wondering what would happen, what he would do, if she said she'd changed her mind.

He started to drop his hand.

"No . . . please." She came across the room then, her hand out, and placed it in his. "I'm just a little . . . nervous, is all. It's been. . ." Her lashes fluttered up and then down again, hiding her expression. "It's been a long time for me, is all, and I'm a little nervous."

Rafe stood there for a moment, staring down at her, wondering if he should let her get away with the half-truths and evasions implicit in her words. *See if you can get her to talk about it,* the woman at the rape crisis center had said. *Don't push her. Let her set the pace.* But how could he do both at the same time? And was now, when she was gearing herself up to get beyond her past, the time to make her confront it?

"Let's see if I can help you relax a little." He lifted her hand to his lips for a brief kiss and let it go, leaving her standing there as he turned and crouched down in front of the clock radio on the bedside table. "Some soft music," he said as he tuned in a country station and turned it down low. "Soft lights." He turned off everything but the bathroom light, leaving the door partially open so the bedroom was clothed in shadows. "Then we both take off our shoes and get comfortable." He sat down on the edge of the bed and tugged off his boots, pretending not to watch as she hesitated and then, reaching out to balance herself against the dresser, bent down and slipped off her sandals.

"Now what?" she asked, turning to him with her strappy shoes still in her hands.

"Now." He took the sandals from her and tossed them behind him, on top of his boots. "We dance," he said, and held out his arms.

She smiled tremulously and came toward him.

He closed his arms around her carefully, stopping himself from crushing her to him the way he wanted to.

The radio station was playing late-night country tunes, soft cowboy laments telling of love lost and found, of hopeless longings and passions fulfilled. They swayed together in time to the music. Not really dancing, because there was no room to dance, just being close and holding each other. His arms were folded across her lower back; hers were folded between them, her hands flat against his chest. They danced to one song and then two and then, somewhere in the third, with Ray Price singing softly about the pleasures two hearts could share and dreams becoming reality with the tenderness of a kiss, Claire slid her arms around Rafe's hard torso and lifted her face to his.

He looked down into her eyes, waiting for her to tell him what she wanted.

"Kiss me," she said softly.

And he smiled and complied, lowering his head to touch his lips to hers. Her mouth was already open this time, her lips parted for the sweet invasion of his tongue. He made her wait, drawing his tongue over the edges of her open lips, wetting them, warming them, teasing them, making tiny forays between them with the tip of his tongue so that his invasion, when it came, would be even sweeter and more welcome. She tasted of cinnamon and coffee—the special Mexican recipe for coffee his mother had served after dinner—and an intoxicating something that was uniquely her.

Her slender body was pliant in his arms. Warm and so deliciously soft against his hardness. He tightened his embrace just a little and slanted his mouth over hers, taking the kiss deeper. A thrill of pleasure—half triumph, half relief—shot through him when she returned both caresses, arching her neck to take the deepening intimacy of his kiss, flattening her hands against his back to hold him closer.

Encouraged, he began to move his hands up and down her back, slowly, sensuously, sliding them over the elegant contours of her shoulders and spine, molding her closer to him as he continued to kiss her. Her hands moved on his back, too, hesitantly at first, with little pressure, as if she were afraid of the response she might evoke. But he continued as he was, still holding her gently, still kissing her with unhurried thoroughness, making her feel sheltered and safe in his arms.

Claire forgot some of her fears and gave in to the curiosity that had driven her to come this far.

He was so big. And so hard. So warm and male. Her hands moved up from the narrowness of his waist, up the long smooth muscles on either side of his spine, unconsciously molding the shape of him, until her palms were curved over the hard muscles covering his shoulder blades.

Rafe groaned, his muscles rippling under her caressing hands, and pulled her even closer. He wanted to pick her up in his arms, to lay her down on the bed and cover her body with his. He wanted to touch her bare skin. He wanted to put his hands on her breasts and feel the nipples tighten with desire. He wanted . . . so many things. And all of them started with her trusting him enough to let him undress her. He grasped a handful of her shirt and tugged gently, pulling it out of her waistband in back.

Claire stiffened but didn't pull away.

Rafe lifted his mouth far enough from hers to speak. "I'm just going to pull your blouse up so I can touch your bare back. Just your back. I won't do anything else without asking you first, all right?"

"Yes." The word was soft and slowly spoken. "All right."

He slipped his hands under the silk material of her shirt, flattening his palms just above the waistband of her chinos. "Okay?"

"Uh-huh."

She sounded breathless. Whether from fear or excitement, he couldn't tell. He moved his hand up higher, caressing her smooth, bare skin the same way he had caressed her through her blouse. Up and down her spine, slowly, repeatedly, praising the softness and silkiness of her with low, heated whispers until she relaxed again.

He pulled a little away from her. "I want to unbutton your blouse. All right?"

Claire hesitated, then swallowed and nodded her head.

"The words, Claire," he demanded softly. "So I can be sure."

"Yes," she said.

He put his hands on the top button of her silk shirt. "You can stop me anytime you want," he said before he started. "Just one word, *no,* and I'll stop." He waited a moment, in case she wanted to say anything and then started slowly unbuttoning her blouse.

The buttons were tiny and his fingers shook a little, making the job more awkward than it might have been. Claire stood utterly still and silent, with her hands at her sides and her head a little down, watching his fingers as they descended the front of her blouse. She took a shuddering breath, tensing as he finished with the last button and reached up to push the two halves of her blouse aside.

"Stop?" he asked.

Claire took another shuddering breath. "No." The word was softly spoken but unequivocal. "No, don't stop."

He pushed the halves of her blouse aside and reached for the front-opening clasp on her bra. "Stop?"

She was quivering like a Thoroughbred before a race, her breathing coming faster than it had just a moment before. "No."

The soft snick of the clasp as it opened sounded like a cannon shot. She felt the material part as the tension was released and then stop, catching on the curve of her breasts. Rafe hesitated, his fingers hovering at the edges of the material.

"Don't stop," she said, before he could ask.

He brushed the lacy material back, freeing her breasts to his eyes and hands. He sucked in his breath on a low hiss. "I'm going to touch you now," he said, his voice low and gruff. "Just barely, so you can see if you like the way my hands feel on you."

He paused, giving her time to object and then, very gently and carefully, cupped his hands around the soft swell of her breasts. They were fuller than he'd expected them to be. Creamy white in the shadowed light shining around the bathroom door, with light brown areolas the size of half-dollars and velvety brown nipples. His long fingers curled around the outside swell of each breast like a living bra. His thumbs brushed against the inner curves, coming close to the pouting nipples but not quite touching them.

"Your clothes hide how voluptuous you are," he said softly, his eyes heated and intense as he stared at his dark hands moving on her creamy skin. "How perfect."

Claire could feel her heart slamming against the wall of her chest as he caressed her, and wondered if he could feel it, too. There was little fear left in her now, it had been mostly overcome by a breathless, shimmering excitement and a need for more. She hadn't known it was possible to feel this way, to feel this good, to feel desire so powerfully. It coursed through her body, making it taut and eager for whatever he would do next.

"I want to put my mouth on you," Rafe said. "Can I put my mouth on you, Claire?"

"Yes." The word was forced out on a strangled breath.

He bent his head and touched his mouth to her throat, right under her jaw where her pulse pounded against her skin. And then farther down, nuzzling the collar of her blouse out of the way to press his mouth to the place where her neck curved into her shoulder. And then down, lower still, on the fragile skin of her upper chest. And then, finally, his lips brushed against the first curving slope of her breast.

Claire waited, tense and aching, for his mouth to cover her nipple.

"Can I taste your nipple, Claire?"

"Yes." It was almost a plea.

His lips skimmed down the slope of her breast. His tongue darted out and, very lightly, laved her nipple.

Claire jerked as if he had touched a live wire to her flesh.

He drew away from her slightly. "Stop?"

"No," she panted. "No, don't stop."

His tongue came out and circled her nipple. Once, twice, three times, slowly, drawing it out until she thought she would scream.

"Can I suck on you, Claire?"

She lifted her hands, fisting them in his hair and, in the first sexually assertive act of her life, pulled his head to her breast. *"Yes!"*

Rafe would have shouted with jubilation and triumph if his mouth hadn't been full of her sweet, succulent breast. He sucked on her strongly, instead, making her shiver and arch into his hands.

"I want to take your blouse and bra all the way off," he murmured long moments later, and she helped him remove it.

"I want to take off my shirt and feel your breasts against my bare chest," he said, and she helped him remove that, too, reaching up to unsnap the fastenings of his western-style shirt with hands that shook much more than a little.

When they were both bare from the waist up, he put his hands on her waist and brought their torsos together. The soft feminine fullness of her pressed against the hardness and hairiness of his wide chest to the unutterable delight of them both. He ran his hands up and down her spine, over her shoulders and arms and then back again, finally cupping her head in his palms to tilt it back and plunder her mouth more thoroughly than he had dared before.

His kiss was blatantly carnal and hot and wet. His tongue plunged into her mouth for a long, leisurely taste and then withdrew, slowly, only to plunge back in again.

Claire panted and opened her mouth wider, pressing herself against him in fierce and unabashed desire. There was nothing of the cool sophisticate left in her now. Nothing of Hollywood's notorious Ice Queen. Nothing of the fear that had paralyzed her for so long.

Rafe skimmed his hands downward again, over her shoulders and bare silky back to the leather belt still clasped around her waist. He pulled his mouth a little away from hers. "Can I unbuckle this?"

"Yes."

"And push off your pants?"

"Yes."

"And your panties? Can I take them off, too?"

"Yes."

"Can I touch you, Claire?" he asked when she was naked.

"Where?" she said breathlessly.

He slid his palms over her bare bottom. "Here," he said, and squeezed gently.

"Yes."

He brushed one finger over the thatch of dark, silky hair at the base of her belly. "And here."

"Yes."

"And—" he let his finger trail down between her legs for just a moment "—here."

"Yes," she panted breathlessly. Her fingernails were digging into his shoulders, but neither of them noticed it.

With one hand riding the small of her back, he turned his other hand, palm up, and inserted it between her legs.

Claire's bones melted and she thought she would faint.

"You're wet for me," Rafe breathed, his voice heavy with the satisfaction of having brought her to this.

"Am I?"

"Mmm," he crooned. "And soft. Soft as butter." He moved his hand, stroking her.

She started to tremble.

"And swollen." Another soft movement of his hand had her tremors increasing until she was shaking like a leaf in a strong wind. "Can I put my fingers inside you, Claire?"

She sagged against him. "I won't be able to stay upright if you do that."

"That's all right. I'll hold you up. Can I?"

She closed her eyes and whimpered. "Yes."

He bent one long finger, curling it up from his enveloping palm and entered her.

She gasped and shuddered, her whole body quaking in response.

"Good?"

"Yes. Oh, yes!"

He pushed his finger deeper inside her and her knees buckled. He caught her around the waist with his other arm.

"Do you want the rest of it, Claire?" he breathed raggedly. "Do you want to take this all the way?" If she said no, he'd just kill himself right here and now. "Do you want me to make love to you?"

"Yes," she murmured, her voice just as ragged as his.

He turned with her clasped against him and took the two steps necessary to bring them to the edge of the bed. Raising his knee, he placed it on the mattress and started to lower her below him to the bed, reaching down to rip open his fly as he did so.

Claire's whole body stiffened with sudden, unthinking rejection.

Instantly Rafe turned in midmotion, falling so that his back was to the bed and she was on top of him. They bounced once, lightly, and he let his hands fall wide, spread out on either side of him.

"I've changed my mind," he announced.

Leery, Claire pushed herself up to look at him. "Changed your mind?"

"I think *you*—" he manufactured a sly, sexy grin to hide his fear that he'd frightened her again, turning her off with his unthinking choice of sexual positions "—should make love to *me*."

She sat upright, seemingly unaware that she was straddling him. "Me make love to you?"

"You've been calling the shots all along here. I think you should continue to call them." He reached out with one hand and touched her breast lightly, hoping to re-kindle the passion that had died such a sudden death when he started to come down on top of her. She squirmed slightly under his caress, making him hope that, maybe, it hadn't died after all.

"Do you want to make love to me this way, Claire?" He thrust upward with his hips, making her bounce. "*With* me?"

She looked down at him from her perch atop his hips, speculation and curiosity growing in her blue eyes. The fear that had almost been stirred up again disappeared as she realized the possibilities of their respective positions—and the freedom it allowed her. A slow, sexy smile, the first of its kind he had seen on her face, curved her perfect cherry-red lips.

"Yes," she said. "I want to make love with you." She leaned forward and put her hands on his bare chest. "Show me how."

"First," he said, crooking a finger at her, "you have to come down here and kiss me into insensibility again. Yes, just like that," he murmured a few long, sweet moments later. "And then you have to touch me here." He guided her hands over his chest. "Yes, that's it. And here." He pushed her hand a little farther down his body. "And—ah!"

"Here?" she said as she lightly touched the distended head of his shaft where it showed in the half-open fly of his jeans.

"Maybe not there," he said, pulling her hand away. "Not right now, anyway. That part of me wants to be inside you too much," he said. "Will you take me inside you, Claire?"

"Yes," she said, and helped him push his jeans down his long legs.

He stayed her hand for a moment, retrieving a foil packet from his pocket before he let her push his jeans completely out of the way. He unrolled the condom onto his near-to-bursting length and then held out his hand, balancing her as she swung her leg over his prone form. He reached down between them, holding himself steady as she slowly lowered herself onto him. He could see the lingering traces of fear in her eyes, despite her passion and her determination to go through with what she'd begun. He set his hands on her waist, halting her slow descent onto his turgid flesh.

"You can stop me anytime, Claire," he said, and hoped it was true. "Just say the word and I'll stop."

Claire took the hands on her waist and drew them up to cover her breasts. "I don't want to stop you," she said, biting her lip, and sank down on him.

They were both utterly still for a moment. Claire closed her eyes, savoring the exquisite sensation of being filled at last, of *wanting* to be filled, of being filled by him. Rafe's eyes stayed determinedly open, watching intently for any signs of distress or discomfort or fear that might mar what he desperately wanted to be a wonderful experience for her.

And then she began to move on him—awkwardly, tentatively, eagerly—and the testosterone began raging through his blood, obliterating every thought and sensation, save one. *Completion.* For both of them.

He slid his hands to her hips, spanning them, showing her the movement and the rhythm that would bring them both to ultimate joy. When she had caught it, reveling in it, he moved one hand down her stomach to the damp thatch of hair between her slender thighs.

"Can I touch you, Claire?" he asked raggedly, still playing their game.

"Yes," she breathed, enraptured by all the new and delicious sensations coursing through her. "Please."

And he did. Softly, sweetly, thoroughly, drawing her inexorably toward complete fulfillment. She cried out when rapture claimed her, overwhelmed and surprised by the intensity of the feeling.

Rafe held her hips hard, holding himself deep and unmoving inside her, watching the ecstasy on her face with an expression of awe and triumph on his.

"I d-didn't know," she stammered, when she could speak again. "I didn't know." Tears of joy and relief glistened on her cheeks. "I didn't think I could," she said.

Unbearably touched, unbearably aroused, Rafe reached up and put his hands on either side of her face. Gently he pulled her down to him. "Of course you can, baby," he said, kissing away her tears. "Of course you can."

"I didn't know," she said again. "Thank you, Rafe." She sighed and pressed her mouth to his.

His hands tightened on either side of her head then, holding her lips pressed against his as he fought for control. And then he sighed raggedly and gave it up. His lips opened wide over hers, his tongue invading and claiming the sweetness of her mouth. His hands slid down from her head, over her shoulders and back, and clamped onto her hips, holding them as he thrust upward, trying to get as deep inside her as he could.

She cried out against his mouth when her second climax took her. He swallowed the sound and then gave it back, following her into the fiery conflagration they'd created with a muffled shout of triumph and joy.

LATER, AS THEY LAY together in the quiet aftermath, Rafe held her and wondered if *now* was the time to ask her about the rape. She'd confronted her fears and, he thought, conquered them for the most part. She was feeling safe and secure. There might never be a more propitious time for her to tackle her past.

"Claire?" he said softly.

"Hmm?" Her voice was soft and dreamy with contentment.

"Do you think you can tell me about the rape now?"

Claire stiffened beside him. "Rape?" she said, trying to sound as if she had no idea what he was talking about. "What rape?"

"Yours."

"I don't know what you're talking about." She tried to pull away from him but he wouldn't let her. "I've never been raped."

"Were you sexually abused as a child, then?"

"No," she said, sounding truly indignant. "Never."

"Then what, Claire? I know something happened to you. Something that made you freeze up inside. Pierce told me I was one of only three men you've ever shown even the mildest interest in and—"

"Pierce has a big mouth," she snapped. "And I already told you, I'm fastidious about whom I get involved with."

"You were shaking like a leaf the first time I kissed you. Hell, the first three times I kissed you. And you were as skittish as a convent-bred virgin tonight."

"Nerves," she said. "I told you it'd been a long time for me."

"Nerves, hell! You nearly bolted when I tried to get on top of you. You were raped," he said, wondering if the woman at the rape crisis center would construe his insistence on the truth as "pushing" her.

"I was not ra—"

He put his hand over her mouth, stopping the words, and she went wild. She kicked out and her hands came up, clawing at his. He let go of her immediately, but not before he'd felt her fingernails scoring down the back of his right hand and her knee connecting painfully with his ribs. She scrambled backward across the bed, her eyes wild and frightened, her breathing fast and erratic.

"Claire, honey, take it easy." He sat up and reached for her, intent on offering comfort.

"Don't touch me."

"I won't touch you. See?" He held up his hands like a man who'd suddenly had a gun pointed at him. "My hands are right here. I won't touch you. All right?" He lowered his hands carefully. "Just tell me about it, baby."

She shook her head. "There's nothing to tell."

"There is," Rafe insisted, knowing that making her talk about it was the right thing to do. She'd kept it inside her for too long. "He put his hand over your mouth, didn't he?"

"Who?"

"The man who raped you. He put his hand over your mouth to keep you from screaming. And then he crawled on top of you and raped you."

"He didn't rape me! How many times do I have to tell you that?"

"Then what did he do?"

"He . . ." Her lips began to tremble pathetically; her eyes began to fill. "He . . ."

"Come on, baby, tell me about it. It won't start to get better until you do."

"It will never get better. Never." Her eyes overflowed, sending hot tears cascading down her ivory cheeks. She wrapped her arms around her middle and curled into the pain. "Never, never, never . . ."

Rafe couldn't stand it. He eased closer to her, carefully, stealthily, and reached out to take her in his arms. She fought him for a moment, fiercely, but her strength was no match for his and she wanted, so badly, to be comforted. Needed to be held and rocked and told it was going to be all right. Rafe dragged her into his lap and held her tight, rocking her back and forth, crooning mindless endearments and assurances into her hair as she curled up in his arms like a frightened child and sobbed out her pain against the reassuring strength of his bare shoulder.

He wondered savagely why the hell there had been no one to hold her after it had happened. No one to tell her it would be all right. To urge her to get counseling to help her deal with it. From what he'd gathered, neither one of her parents were much good, as parents went. But where were those brothers of hers? Why hadn't they hunted down the pervert who had hurt her and made sure he never hurt another woman again?

"Better now?" he said when she had quieted to occasional shuddering sighs. "Want to blow your nose?"

She nodded against his neck. "I n-need a drink of w-water, too."

"Okay." He eased her off his lap and onto the bed, reaching down to pull the covers up around her. "You stay right here and I'll get it for you."

He was back in a minute, with a box of tissues and a glass of water and a cold, wet washcloth. He offered her the tissues to blow her nose, and then tilted up her chin and smoothed the cold washcloth over her hot face and throat with tender, loving strokes. She accepted his ministrations as docilely as a child, handing back the glass of water with a quiet little thank-you.

He took it and put it on the bedside stand, and pulled back the covers and got into bed beside her. She cuddled against him when he put his arm around her, settling her head on his shoulder as naturally as if she had done it every night of her life.

"Want to tell me about it now?" he asked.

She sighed and began speaking to the shadowed ceiling above the bed. "It happened a long time ago. I was still a teenager. And it was somebody I had a crush on." He felt her shrug against him. "Or thought I did. I've never been particularly good at getting a fix on my own emotions. Anyway—" She hurried on before he could address that, and he didn't interrupt her for fear of stopping the healing flow of words. "We were alone together one afternoon and he kissed me. I liked it at first. A lot. I have to admit that. I lay down on the couch with him and let him kiss me and I kissed him back. I didn't even object too much when he put his hand under my sweater. And then, I don't know... something changed. I got scared. I tried to push him off me, to make him stop but he wouldn't listen. He said I'd started it and I had to finish it. That nobody likes a tease. I started to cry and that's when he put his hand over my mouth. It was hard for me to breathe, because I was crying so hard and his hand over my mouth made it worse. And then he pushed my skirt up and tore my panties off and . . . did it. It hurt really bad, but I didn't bleed much so he told me to stop being such a crybaby. Then he kissed me again and told me next time it would be easier because I'd know what to expect. And, maybe, when I got more used to it, he'd teach me a few tricks. I told him I was going to tell my parents that he'd raped me. He was so surprised when I said that." She shook her head against his shoulder. "I'll never forget how surprised he looked. And then he laughed and said they'd never believe me and that even if they did, noth-ing would ever happen except that the tabloids would have a field day with the story. And after I thought about it, I knew he was right."

"You don't think your family would have believed you?" he said, incredulous.

"No . . . I mean, yes, I think they would have. Pierce and Gage, anyway. And my mother. Maybe. But I did go to his trailer. I did have a crush on him. I did kiss him." She laughed soullessly. "He even wore a condom that afternoon because he said he'd already had one paternity suit against him and he wasn't taking a chance on another. So who'd have believed I was raped? I still have a hard time believing it myself."

"No," Rafe said violently. "You were raped. When a woman says no, no matter *when* she says no, and the man still goes ahead with it, it's rape. Especially when the woman is just an inexperienced girl."

"I understand what you're saying," Claire said. "Hey, I've seen Oprah," she added, trying for a little humor. "I even agree with it on an intellectual level but in here—" she touched the area over her heart "—I'm not so sure that it wasn't at least partly my fault."

"It wasn't your fault, dammit! And I want you to stop saying it was." He realized that his hands were clenched on the blankets in a killing grip and he loosened them. It wasn't the hapless blankets he wanted between his fingers, anyway. It was the scrawny neck of the pervert who'd raped Claire. "Who was it?" he asked softly, realizing that, in all her long, painful monologue, she hadn't said.

"It isn't important."

"It is to me."

She shook her head. "I didn't tell anyone then and I'm not going to tell anyone now." She rose up on her elbow to look at him in the dim light. "I want you to promise me that you won't tell anyone, either, Rafe. Not about any of it. Especially my family. It would only hurt Gage and Pierce to hear about it now. They'd blame themselves for not being there or doing some—"

"As well they should!"

"No. Please. I want you to promise me you won't say anything. It's over and done with. And nothing in the world can change it. And, maybe now—" she touched his stubbled cheek, cupping it in her palm "—because of you, I can start to forget it."

Rafe reached up, pressing her palm to his cheek for a moment before sliding it to his mouth. He kissed it deeply, fervently, and then curled his fingers around hers and brought both their hands to rest on his chest. "Go to sleep, now," he crooned softly, easing her head down onto his shoulder with his other hand. "You must be exhausted."

She dropped off almost instantly, exhausted as he had said. Rafe lay awake in the darkness, holding her while she slept, and plotting revenge on the man who had hurt her. True, she hadn't told Rafe who he was, but she had dropped more clues than she knew. The movie world was small and insulated; he'd run into the sorry son of a bitch eventually. Somewhere. Someday. And when he did, he'd make damned sure the perverted bastard rued the day he ever laid a hand on Claire Kingston.

10

THE INSISTENT, FAR-OFF ringing of a telephone woke Claire the next morning, tugging at her consciousness through the layers of sleep and dreams drifting through her mind. She resisted its siren call for a moment, burrowing deeper into her pillow, loath to give up the strange sense of contentment and well-being that enveloped her.

She'd been having such a nice dream!

But the phone rang on relentlessly, demanding to be answered. She reached out, groping blindly for the nightstand in an effort to locate the receiver, and put her hand smack-dab in the middle of what was unmistakably a hairy male chest. There was a man in her bed! She tensed for a moment, and then remembered. Profound relief and thanksgiving flooded through her.

Rafe.

She was in his bed.

In his room.

In his arms.

And sound of the ringing telephone was coming from her room next door.

Being one of those driven people who are constitutionally unable to ignore the imperative summons of a ringing phone, she started to sit up and slide out of her side of the bed. Being one of those people who could ignore just about anything when it suited him, Rafe reached out and wrapped his arm around her bare waist, pulling her back down beside him.

"Let it ring," he said, and snuggled his face into the warm curve of her neck.

"It might be important."

"It might also be a wrong number."

"But—"

"If it's important they'll call back at a more civilized hour."

Claire lifted her head off the pillow, peering over his shoulder at the clock on the nightstand. "What time is it, anyway?"

"Early," Rafe assured her. He made a soft humming noise as he nuzzled his way down her neck. "Very early."

"It can't be all that early. The sun is already— Rafe!" She jerked as she felt his lips graze her nipple. "What are you doing?"

His exaggerated sigh of frustration was warm against the sensitive skin of her breast. "I'm *trying* to interest you in a little morning roll in the hay. But—" he looked up at her through a thick veil of lashes "—since you have to ask, it's obvious my technique needs work." He rolled onto his back, pulling her half on top of him, and put his hand behind her head. "Come 'ere," he whispered, and brought her mouth down to his.

His morning kiss was deep and sweet. Languid and lavish and loving. And she was melting inside when he let her up for air, making it obvious to Claire, at least, that his technique didn't need any work at all.

"How are you feeling this morning?" he murmured, his eyes tender and concerned as he stared up into her face.

"Fine."

"No bad aftereffects?"

She shook her head.

"And you don't hate me for making you talk about it?"

She smiled and raised an imperious eyebrow. "Does it look as if I hate you?"

Rafe grinned. What other woman, he marveled, could manage that adorably superior expression while stark naked and sprawled all over a man's chest? "Then could I interest you in that little roll in the hay I mentioned?"

She blushed, giving him his answer.

His grin widened, becoming predatory and male, and he rolled back to his side so that they lay face-to-face. He was careful, as he kissed her, not to push her onto her back or loom over her too heavily. He ran his hand down her side, over the inward sloping curve of her narrow waist, to the gentle flare of her hip, along the length of her smooth, silky thigh, to her knee. He curled his fingers around the back of it and pulled it up and over his hip, opening her to his touch.

She sighed as his fingers whispered up the back of her thigh, and then whimpered softly as they trailed over the hot, silky folds of her. She tilted her hips forward, pressing them against his hard male shaft, as his fingers teased her feminine cleft from behind. Rafe groaned and shifted and pulled her leg higher on his hip, entering her in one smooth motion.

They smiled and began to move against each other. The mood was warm and sweet between them, the loving languid and deliciously drowsy. They kissed. Deep, soft, wet kisses that went on forever. They touched, exploring each other's bodies with delicate fingertips and smooth palms, stroking, soothing, celebrating, beguiled and enchanted by the differences between them. They murmured and sighed and exclaimed softly, letting the passion build in whispers and gentle caresses.

Until, finally, Rafe's control came to end. And, even then, he remembered not to roll on top of her. He slid his hands down to her hips instead, holding her, bracing her slender body for a more vigorous possession. He thrust against her forcefully, powerfully, but oh-so-carefully, until she caught fire, too, and began to answer him with driving thrusts of her own.

The telephone in her room began to ring again but Claire didn't hear it. The pounding of blood in her ears was louder, the beat of her heart more insistent, the thrust of her lover's hips against hers more compelling by far. Claire arched her body like a bow and let it take her.

"I THINK WE'RE GOING to need to establish a few ground rules before the rest of the crew gets here," Claire said as they sat eating breakfast in the Flat Rock Café.

"Sure," Rafe agreed, thinking she was talking about rules pertaining to life on a movie set. "What did you have in mind?"

"Nothing earth-shattering." Claire took a sip of her tea and made a mental note to have Robert send her a supply of her favorite blend. She doubted the local Piggly Wiggly stocked Chinese mint. "Just a few basic parameters to keep things running smoothly between us."

Rafe paused with his coffee cup halfway to his mouth. "Us?"

"You and me," she explained.

"You want to establish ground rules between you and me?"

Claire lifted an eyebrow at him. For some reason he didn't think it was quite so adorable as he had earlier that morning. "Isn't that what I just said?"

"Personal or professional?"

"Is there a difference?"

"I was certainly under the impression there was. Apparently, I missed something." He set his coffee cup down with a sharp click. "Maybe you'd better start this discussion over."

"I don't know what you're getting so upset about. I just—"

"I'm not upset."

Claire's expression told him what she thought of that lie—and his interruption. "I just thought that, to forestall any gossip on the set or in the tabloids, we should establish a few rules about our relationship."

"Such as?"

"Such as no public displays of . . . affection, no being seen going in and out of each other's room at all hours, no long lunches that aren't lunches. That sort of thing."

Rafe gave her a hard look. "Why? Are you ashamed of what we do together?"

"No," she said, shocked that he would even suggest such a thing. "No, of course not! I just don't want to give anyone anything to gossip about, that's all."

"Gossip is an unavoidable fact of the movie industry," Rafe reminded her. "I'd think you'd know that by now."

"Yes, I know. But I'd like to avoid creating any more of it than I absolutely have to."

"Why?" he asked again.

"Because *Desperado* is very special to me. And because I want it to fail or succeed on its own merits, without being colored by what is or isn't going on between its producer and director, that's why."

"Any particular reason?" he asked, although he thought he might know.

Claire hesitated and then plunged ahead, deciding to trust him with another part of herself. "Ever since I started working as a producer with Kingston Productions, I've had to fight the perception that I'm only here on sufferance. That I only got the job because my family's name is on the door. That was true, at first. I was totally green when I started and I made some mistakes. But I learned from them and I've become a damn fine producer. I've been responsible for some terrific movies."

"And some people in Hollywood still think you're just your mother's errand girl."

"Yes."

"And you're hoping *Desperado* will prove you're not. That's why no one else in your family is involved in it in any way, isn't it?"

"Yes. I want to do it all on my own. And I want people to *know* I've done it on my own."

Rafe could understand that. Sort of. After all, he didn't want *his* efforts on the picture tarnished by rumors that he'd gotten the director's spot by sleeping with the boss. But that didn't explain why *she* didn't want anyone to know about their relationship. The fact that she was sleeping with him wasn't going to affect anyone's opinion of her abilities as a producer.

"That's pretty thin, Claire," he said suspiciously, his old insecurity rearing its head.

"Thin?"

"Hollywood isn't going to judge your contributions to this picture on the basis of whether or not you're sleeping with me." He skewered her with a look. "So what's your real reason for wanting to pretend there's nothing between us?"

"That *is* my reason."

"Claire . . ."

"I just don't want any gossip about us."

"Why?" If she was ashamed of him he wanted to know it now.

"Because . . ." She shrugged uneasily and looked down, tearing her whole wheat toast into shreds.

Rafe steeled himself to hear an unpleasant truth.

"Because it's all so new to me," she said finally. "Because I don't want our...relationship," she decided, not knowing what else to call it, "to be dissected and analyzed and smirked about in the national press." She looked up at him, then, her eyes wide and clear and honest. "Is that so hard for you to understand? That I'm a little...shy about it?"

"No," Rafe said. "No, that's not hard to understand at all." He sighed. "All right," he said, resigning himself to the public pretense that everything between him and Claire was strictly business. "What were those ground rules again?"

"RAFE. YOO-HOO. Rafe Santana." The feminine voice was high-pitched and sugary sweet, with a thick West Texas drawl.

Rafe looked up from the discussion he was having with Becky Ward over the sketches she'd done to illustrate her ideas for the main interiors of *Desperado*. They'd already decided on all of the outdoor locations and had found the perfect place to represent Josh's rundown farmhouse. But Tony Banks, the location manager, was still visiting local homes in hopes of finding one or two to stand in for Molly's posh, upper-class residence. But they were up against the wire with the shooting schedule and if Tony didn't find them, and get the necessary contracts signed within the next two days, Becky was going to instruct her crew to go ahead and build the sets in the barn they'd rented. And then R. J. Bennington, the set decorator, was going to have to spend a fortune to furnish those sets. It wasn't a problem designed to put any director working under a tight deadline and an even tighter budget in the best of moods, especially when he was already sliding toward cranky to begin with.

The last thing he needed was another interruption in his work schedule, Rafe thought, looking toward the owner of the voice with a frown. And the last interruption he needed was *her*.

"It's me, Laura Lyn Parker," she said, giving him her best smile. "Well, Parker-Moore, now. Don't ever say you don't remember me," she said with a flirtatious little laugh. "Not after all we've been to each other."

Oh, he remembered her all right. Laura Lyn Parker, the belle of Flat Rock, Texas, and the girl who'd given him his first lesson in the perfidy of a certain type of woman.

There'd been a time when she could make his heart beat faster and his palms sweat just by walking into a room. Even after she'd dumped him, he'd continued to moon over her for longer than he liked to remember. He'd spent many a lonely night out on an oil rig in the Gulf, dreaming of the day he'd return to Flat Rock, a roaring success, and sweep pretty little Laura Lyn right off her pretty little feet. Before dumping her right on her equally pretty little ass, in as public a way as he could manage.

That particular dream had spurred his ambitions for several years but, as a goal, it hardly seemed worth the time he'd spent thinking about it. Even though he could tell, just by looking at her, that he could accomplish it with very little effort. Laura Lyn was ripe for plucking.

"Excuse me for a minute, Laura Lyn," he said with barely restrained politeness, and turned away from her. He threw his clipboard down on top of the art director's sketches and roared for his production manager. "Claire!" he bellowed. "Claire, where the hell are you?"

"I'm right here, Rafe," she said, hurrying up to him without seeming to hurry at all, "there's no need to holler at me."

"I wasn't hollering at you. I was hollering for you. There's a difference."

"Really?" She lifted her brow at him, giving him a frosty look meant to put him firmly in his place.

It made him grin. "Yeah, really." He lowered his voice seductively. "And if you'll come to my trailer, I'll explain the difference in detail."

Claire ignored that, as she ignored all his barbs and innuendos. In public, they were back to the Ice Queen and the Upstart Director and, so far, the director was losing most of their encounters. In the two weeks since they'd started shooting, there hadn't been a breath of scandal to even suggest that the link between them was anything other than strictly professional.

It was driving Rafe crazy.

Because he was beginning to feel the overwhelming need to stake his claim on Claire publicly.

Not that he'd said anything as Neanderthal as that to her. He hadn't even really admitted it to himself—not out loud. But the thoughts of unassailable, unquestionable possession were there. Constantly. And growing more all-encompassing by the day. And night. Especially by night.

And most especially when he began to notice Dax Wyatt hovering around her like a shadow every chance he got. Dax was a perennial Hollywood golden boy, only eight or so years older than Claire, with thick, sun-streaked, wheat-colored hair, blue eyes that were often called "deliciously roguish" by the tabloids and lots of perfect white teeth. He had a Sean Penn sneer that enabled him to play petulant bad boys convincingly, and an aw-shucks air of innocence, when he cared to project it, that made those bad boys seem as if they hid hearts of gold beneath the dross. All of which made him perfect for the part of Josh. Which was unfortunate, really, because Rafe was starting to dislike him.

Claire had expressed an aversion to their star's particular brand of charm, but lately she didn't seem to mind so much when he came sniffing around her. Rafe hadn't had to rescue her from Dax's oily clutches even once since shooting began. And, while he was glad that she seemed to have discovered the trick for handling the actor without any undue stress to herself, he couldn't help the niggling little feeling of . . . all right, might as well admit it, he thought... *jealousy* that snaked up his spine whenever he saw the two of them together.

They had the same sort of background. They were in the same business. They'd even done a successful movie together.

And the gossip columnists were having a field day with it.

There hadn't been a whiff of scandal about the affair Claire *was* having with Rafe, but the one she *wasn't* having with Dax Wyatt was all over the tabloids.

"Was there some reason you called me over here?" Claire asked him as he stood there, staring at her with an intent look on his face. "Or did you just want to hear yourself bellow? I do have work to do, you know."

"Work?" he said. "Ah, yes, work. Now I remember." He put his hand on Claire's upper arm and pulled her close, walking her out of the hearing range of the bright-eyed Laura Lyn. "I want you to get rid of her."

"Her, who?"

"The local society maven with the big hair." He jerked his head toward Laura Lyn. "I don't like civilians hanging around my set while I'm trying to work. It ruins my concentration."

"Yes, I can see where it might. She's quite an eyeful." Rafe grunted. "If you like cheerleaders."

Claire looked up at him out of the corner of her eye. "Which Pilar tells me you did, once. Quite a lot, in fact."

"Pilar told you about Laura Lyn?"

"And Iona, and Tiffany, and Bobbi Sue, and Cat—"

Rafe made as if to put his hand over her mouth to stop the litany. It was a measure of Claire's progress that she didn't flinch; it was a measure of Rafe's sensitivity that he drew back before he actually did it.

"So, are you going to get rid of her?"

Claire shook her head. "Can't."

"What do you mean, *can't*? You're the production manager. Go over there and give her some story about how we can't allow non-cast and crew members on the set because of insurance or something. I heard you use that one yesterday on a bunch of autograph hounds."

"Laura Lyn isn't an autograph hound. She's one of our hostesses."

"Hostesses? What hostesses?"

"The Flat Rock Country Club has graciously opened its doors as a recreational facility for our cast and crew while we're here. For a price, of course."

Rafe scowled ferociously.

"Be reasonable, Rafe. I couldn't very well turn them down. They've got the best restaurant in town. And the only swimming pool for miles. Not to mention an air-conditioned recreation hall for the nightly poker game. The crew would have lynched us both if I'd said no just because you carry a mean grudge."

"Well, then, get somebody to give her the grand tour or something as a gesture of our profound appreciation. And then get rid of her."

"Do you have a tour guide in mind?"

Rafe glanced over at the group of actors lolling around in the shade of a cottonwood as they waited for the next scene to be set up. A calculating gleam lit up his hot-coffee eyes. "Give her to Dax Wyatt," he said. "They deserve each other."

"CUT! DAMMIT, CUT!" Rafe hollered.

"Take a break, everyone," Pilar said, anticipating her brother's next command.

The whole morning had been spent shooting the same scene and it hadn't been going well at all. Rafe hadn't ordered even one foot of film printed for the scene yet, which was a measure of his frustration with it. He called his production assistant, then turned around and headed for his on-set office trailer without waiting to see if Claire followed him.

"Fifteen minutes, everyone," Pilar shouted through her bullhorn. "Don't go wandering off."

"That scene still isn't working," Rafe said as Claire stepped into the trailer behind him. He slammed the door closed. "And I'm tired of working with that prima donna writer long-distance. I want you to call K.E.C., whoever the hell he is, and tell him to get his candy-ass on the next flight out here. I want to go over this scene, and a few others, with him personally," he groused, pacing up and down the narrow trailer. "We'll see who will or will not change his precious script."

"Just what, exactly, do you think needs changing now?" Claire asked with deceptive calm. The scene had been reworked twice already and he still wasn't satisfied with it.

"You know very well what needs changing. That scene—" he waved a hand toward the door of the trailer "—isn't working the way it's written and you damn well know it."

"Maybe it's the way you're interpreting it that isn't working," Claire suggested sweetly.

"My interpretation is just fine," he shot back. "It's the writing that stinks. And I want it changed. Now," he demanded.

"You know that 'now' is impossible. I'll have to call the writer tonight and—"

"*Now*," Rafe said. He picked up the telephone and thrust it at her. "And I'll talk to him myself since you seem unable to convey the problem."

"Her," Claire said before she could stop herself.

"What?"

"Her," Claire said through clenched teeth. "The writer is a her."

"Fine. Whatever. Get *her* on the phone then, so I can straighten her out."

"She doesn't need straightening out. What she needs is a director with enough sensitivity to understand the scene as it's written."

"What she *needs* is to start acting like a professional and get her ass on this set to see for herself why this scene isn't working." He thrust the phone into Claire's hand. "So call her," he ordered.

Claire slammed the phone down. "I don't need to call her."

"Don't need—? Dammit, Claire, I said call her," he roared.

"And I said I don't need to call her," she roared back. "Because she's right here."

"What the hell are you talking about?"

"She is me," Claire said furiously. "*I'm* the writer."

Rafe just stared at her, dumbstruck.

"K.E.C. is me," Claire said, thinking he simply didn't understand. "Claire Elise Kingston, backward."

"The writer is you?"

"Yes." Claire nodded emphatically, as if daring him to disbelieve her. "That's right. Me."

"And you've been carrying on this ridiculous charade, letting me think that you had to call some reclusive writer every time I wanted to change one word of the script?"

"Yes."

"*Why*, for God's sake?"

"I didn't want anyone to know," she said, as if it should be perfectly obvious. "I still don't want anyone to know."

"Why?" he said again.

"For the same reason I've been so adamant about gossip. And for the same reason no one in my family is involved in *Desperado*. Because I don't want people saying the only reason it got made was because I wrote it and my family was giving me a break."

"And isn't that the reason?"

She looked at him with wide, hurt eyes. "Don't you think it's any good?"

"Hell, yes, of course it's *good*. I wouldn't have gotten involved in the project if I didn't think it was damn good," he said, dissolving her hurt before it had a chance to take root. "But that doesn't mean it's getting made for that reason. Lots of movies that are no damn good at all get made for all kinds of reasons, including nepotism."

"Well, this movie isn't riding on anyone's coattails. No one in my family knows who the writer is. And I want it to stay that way until after it's been released."

"Fine," Rafe said. "But that scene still needs work."

"I know," Claire admitted, and made an executive decision. "Why don't we call an early lunch? We can have sandwiches in here and rewrite it together. I've heard some of your ideas for the scene—repeatedly—" she added with a grin "—and I think they'll work.

With a little fine tuning from me, of course. Just to keep it true to the characters. What do you say?"

"Aren't you afraid of gossip if we spend the entire lunch break in here together?"

Claire shook her head. "We'll leave the door open."

He put his hand on her arm, stopping her when she would have opened the door.

She looked at him questioningly.

"It's a great screenplay," he said with unassailable certainty. And complete sincerity.

Claire felt a warm glow all through her at his praise.

"COMING," CLAIRE HOLLERED, getting up from the makeshift desk to answer the knock on her motel-room door.

This wearing of three hats—four, she thought, if you counted her new role as a lover—was getting to be a strain. She'd been up since before the crack of dawn, sneaking back from Rafe's motel room to hers. She'd fielded two calls from a young, inexperienced director who was filming on location in New York and the minute they wrapped on *Desperado*—which, God willing, would be in less than a week—she was going to have to fly out there to personally hold his hand. Her mother had been keeping the fax machine humming for the past ten days, firing off missives from Paris about the newest Kingston production, *Man About Town*, which they hoped to film with Richard Gere in the title role. And Robert, bless his organized little heart, had express-mailed her the latest status reports on four other projects currently in the works. All of which had to be taken care of before she reported to work on the set of *Desperado* at eight o'clock.

"Come on in, Rafe," she said, turning the lock before she looked to see who it was. "I'll be off the phone in just a minute."

It took a couple of minutes more than a few, and when she finally turned around after a long and protracted conversation with a film editor she would never hire again, it was to find Dax Wyatt sitting in the middle of her bed with his feet up, reading her latest copy of *Variety* and drinking coffee from a disposable cup. She warned herself not to lose her legendary cool. She could handle this; she'd been handling it for the past month. "Is there something I can do for you, Dax?" she said politely, eyeing him as if he were a snake that had crawled in from outside and curled up on her bed.

He held up a plastic cup. "I brought you coffee."

"That's very thoughtful of you," she said. "But I drink tea." She waited a beat. "Is there anything else?"

"Have you seen the latest tabloids?"

"No," she said shortly. "I read that trash as rarely as possible."

"You should read it more often. You're a featured player."

"Me?"

"Well." He gave her his patented aw-shucks grin, the one that was supposed to make her fall at his feet. "You and me."

Claire's gaze turned several degrees colder. "There is no you and me."

"According to this, there is." He picked up one of the tabloids he'd apparently brought into the room with him and held it out to her.

After a moment's hesitation, Claire reached out and took it.

It was the usual tabloid trash. A bold headline, Romance Rekindled! with pictures to prove it. Pictures that had obviously been taken on the set of *Desperado*. Pictures that Dax had quite obviously created the opportunities for. The two of them, standing in the doorway of a trailer; she remembered him stopping her to "discuss" a problem with one of his scenes. And the one of him leaning over the back of her chair in the library, looking as if he were nibbling on her ear; she'd used the break between scenes to prepare a fax to send to Robert when Dax suddenly leaned over her. She'd gotten up and walked away a minute later. The rest were more of the same, except for two.

Those were photographs of her and Dax on the set of *The Deceivers*, taken nearly eight years ago. They were in character in one, dressed and posed as the star-crossed young lovers they had played. The other picture was a candid shot, taken in the chow line in front of the caterers truck when she was still stupid enough to think she'd had a crush on him.

The story was sickening. A tale of young lovers torn apart by Claire's parents; hints that her withdrawal from the public eye had been caused by a broken heart; the insinuation that her Ice Queen image had been deliberately cultivated to protect that fragile organ from more pain; speculation that the heart was now in the process of being mended by the not-so-young lovers after being reunited on the set of another movie.

Claire lifted her gaze from the paper and stared at him with an icy white-hot rage. "Why?"

"It's great publicity, Claire."

"It's a lie."

Dax shrugged. "A little white one, maybe. You did have a crush on me. And I did break your heart."

Claire was suddenly shaking with anger. "You didn't break my heart, you bastard. You raped me."

"Oh, Jesus, Claire, are you still trying to sell that story? You were a hot little number who could hardly wait to give it to me."

"I was an eighteen-year-old girl who thought she was in love."

"Yeah, well." He shrugged. "That's what I said, wasn't it?"

Claire threw the paper at him. "Get out," she growled, her voice thick with disgust.

Dax stood up. "You're still a hot little number, Claire," he said, and reached for her.

Claire froze as his hands closed over her shoulders. *Oh, God, it's happening again,* she thought, suddenly paralyzed with terror. She opened her mouth to scream but her vocal cords refused to work. *Oh, please, God, don't let it happen again.*

Dax laughed softly. "And you still can't wait to give it to me, can you?" he gloated, obviously taking her terrified stillness for acquiescence. He pulled her closer and bent his head. The thought of actually having his mouth on hers spurred her to instinctive action and she backed away. He followed her, crowding her backward like a sheepdog herding a terrified lamb. "Such an eager little girl," he said, chuckling, and pushed her down onto the bed.

Her hands flailed out helplessly, one of them brushing against the open container of coffee he'd left on the nightstand. She grabbed at it blindly, ignoring the hot liquid that splashed on her fingers and, in one terrified, desperate effort to save herself, threw it at him. *"Get out!"* she screamed, finding her voice at last.

It hit him in the chest, sending the hot liquid spraying in all directions. His handsome face twisted. "You bitch," he growled, and lunged at her.

Claire brought her knees up and kicked out with every ounce of strength she possessed. *"I'm not going to let you do it to me again!"* she screamed. Her feet caught him in the stomach and sent him crashing against the wall with enough force to bring the hunting print that decorated it crashing to the floor.

It also brought Rafe crashing in from the room next door. "What the hell—" he began but the tableau that greeted his eyes told its own story. With a roar of rage, he reached down and grabbed Dax by the back of his shirt. Hauling him to his feet with a berserker's strength, Rafe cocked back his arm, prepared to put an end to Dax Wyatt's golden good looks forever.

Claire threw herself forward and grabbed his arm. "Don't hit him, Rafe."

Maddened, he tried to shake her off so he could finish what he'd started. No man touched *his* woman without paying the price!

"For God's sake, don't hit him!" Claire said, clinging like a limpet to his arm. "He's only got four scenes left to shoot."

Rafe made a strangled sound. "Scenes?" he said, incredulous. "This clown attacked you—" he shook Dax by the back of the neck, like a mastiff would shake a terrier "—and you're worried about how many scenes he's got left?"

"If you mess up his face, we'll go over budget while he recuperates," she said and, incredibly, she was smiling.

Laughing.

Some of Rafe's murderous anger left him.

She was laughing!

"Well, can I at least sucker-punch him a couple of times?" he asked.

11

THEY THREW DAX outside like a piece of trash, Claire holding the door open, Rafe running him out with one hand on his shirt collar and the other on his belt. He stumbled against one of the pillars holding up the porch overhang and managed, barely, to stay upright. Or as upright as a man who was grasping his manhood and gasping for every breath he could. Claire's kick had caught him low in the stomach, knocking the wind out of him and catching his penis with the heel of her foot, thus rendering Rafe's aid appreciated but unnecessary.

"I'll see your asses in court over this," Dax gasped.

"It will be our pleasure," Rafe told him, and slammed the door.

Claire launched herself at him like a rocket, knocking him back against the closed door.

Rafe closed his arms around her and held on tight. "Claire, honey, are you all right? Did that bastard hurt you after all? Oh, baby, don't cry. Don't cry."

She lifted her face from his neck to show him she wasn't crying. Far from it. The strangled sounds coming from her throat were wild whoops of laughter. The tears squeezing out from the corners of her eyes were tears of relief and joy.

"Oh, God," she said, nearly doubled over with mirth. "Did you see his face? Did you? He was so surprised. He didn't expect me to fight back. But I did," she exulted. I *did!*"

"You sure as hell did, baby." Rafe scooped her up in his arms and began to twirl her around the room, sharing in her joy and triumph. "You sure as hell did."

They reeled drunkenly for a moment, and then Rafe tripped and stumbled and they went tumbling to the bed. Claire twisted in his arms, turning to twine her body around his, and brought her mouth down on his. The kiss was hard and fierce and wild.

"Make love to me, Rafe," she demanded. "Make love to me right now."

He hesitated. She'd just been attacked, and even though she seemed to have weathered it amazingly well, her reaction could be the result of some kind of shock.

"*Now*," she demanded, and brought her lips down on his again.

He wrapped his arms around her and held her close, returning her kiss with all the intensity and furor with which she gave it, trying mightily to gentle her before he lost control and gave her what she thought she wanted.

Claire raised her head. "I'm not wounded or in shock," she said, staring down into his eyes. "I'm not some injured little bird or a wild calico cat you have to tame with gentleness. Not anymore. I'm a woman who's just confronted her past. And won. And I want to celebrate that victory with the man I love in the best way I know how."

"My God. Claire." Emotion overwhelmed Rafe, making it impossible for him to form complete sentences. "Claire."

"Tell me later," she said. And kissed him.

They rolled over the bed in a heated, frantic swelter of desire. Kissing. Touching. Pulling at clothes to kiss and touch what lay below the restricting cloth. Moaning deeply as fingers found and caressed. Groaning as palms cupped. Panting. Aching. Wanting.

"Now," Claire said, pulling him on top of her. "Oh, please, *now*, Rafe."

For the first time, he was on top when he entered her. She arched beneath him. Straining. Gasping. Glorying in his thorough, passionate, powerful possession of her willing body. The first fiery climax wasn't nearly enough. For either of them. Rafe wanted her to have it all. Every shudder, every sigh, every glorious, gutwrenching sensation, every explosive release she'd been denied while the Ice Queen reigned.

He reared back on his haunches and hooked his arms under her legs. Leaning forward, balancing himself on his hands, he thrust into her heavily, slowly, making her moan and tremble and, finally, scream with the intensity of her release.

His own claimed him then, more powerful, more potent than anything he'd ever felt before. It seemed to begin at the top of his head and the soles of his feet at the same time and race, crashing, like two bull elephants, to explode in a glorious rush as he poured himself into her.

They collapsed together—hot, sweaty, trembling—in a heap of blissful satisfaction.

It was a few minutes before Rafe could steady his breathing enough to talk but, when he did, he said all the words she wanted to hear.

"You were magnificent," he said. "Utterly, completely magnificent. And I love you. Utterly and completely. And as soon as I can move again, we're going to hightail it to Las Vegas and get married."

"But—"

Rafe put his finger to her lips. "But nothing. I don't care if the movie goes over schedule. I don't care if it goes over budget. I don't care if the tabloids say I got the job because of nepotism. Or because I'm sleeping with you. I only care about you. So—" he took his finger from her mouth "—what do you say to that?"

"Yes," she said.

Epilogue

THE TABLOIDS HAD a field day, reporting on the charges of assault and counterassault. Reports of shooting delays and budget overruns made the press as gleeful as children on Christmas morning. Allegations of nepotism and sexual harassment were flung around with abandon. Rumors of a quickie wedding at a drive-through Las Vegas wedding chapel were reported but never confirmed—and were later contradicted by a small private family ceremony held in Pierce Kingston's backyard.

Blissfully ensconced in a secret Kingston hideaway snuggled in the small town of Mammoth in the southern Sierras, the newlyweds ignored it all.

DESPERADO WAS PREVIEWED four months later in gala Hollywood style, after a hurry-up edit—in which the director *did* get the final cut—to release it in time for the Christmas season. The tabloid reporters and legitimate critics turned out in force.

The tabloid journalists came in anticipation of the fireworks sure to ensue when the producer, director and male star showed up for the same party. Most of them were hoping for nothing less than bloodshed. Much to their dismay, all parties involved were distressingly civilized, although speculation was rife when Dax Wyatt showed up with his nose bandaged and his eyes bruised. The next day's headlines reported the cause as a car accident, a bungled nose job and violent contact with some unspecified object, depending on which tabloid you read.

The critics were there because they'd heard rumors that one of the Kingstons had actually written the screenplay and everyone wanted to be the first to trash it in print. The newspaper critics all hated it: mawkishly sentimental, was the nicest thing said. On television, Gene Siskel gave it a definite thumbs-down but Roger Ebert thought it deserved a tentative thumbs-up for its uplifting ending and Christine Bishop's terrific performance as Molly.

The movie premiered Christmas week, grossing an amazing $29.1 million its first weekend, surpassed only by Macaulay Culkin's Christmas offering. According to *Entertainment Weekly*, it was still one of the top ten grossers twelve weeks later, proving that, while the critics may have hated it, the movie-going public lapped it up. The sweet little love story had—in the Hollywood vernacular—extremely long "legs."

It was passed over for a Golden Globe award but garnered a People's Choice for Best Picture. And what the Academy would do at Oscar time was anybody's guess.

RAFE AND CLAIRE sat together in the first row of the Dorothy Chandler Pavilion on Oscar night. Sitting on

Claire's left was the newly svelte Nikki, who'd given birth to a baby girl just two short months ago, and Pierce, who was up for an Oscar for Best Actor in a Leading Role for his portrayal of ladies' man, Matt Gleason, in *Made For Each Other*. Not being up for any awards—and, so, not needing easy access to the stage— Tara and Gage sat just behind them with Rafe's sister, Pilar, who was doing her best not to gawk at all the movie stars.

To Rafe's right was his mother, Dolores, beaming with pride and looking absolutely radiant in a red St. Laurent that made the most of her dark coloring.

The rest of the Santana clan was watching at home, gathered at Inez and Miguel's ranch house for an Oscar night party.

Elise Gage was watching via satellite in Paris, France, ready to send a congratulatory cable if any project or person connected with Kingston Productions won.

Barry Kingston was in Istanbul, shooting a movie and romancing his twenty-two-year-old leading lady.

On stage, Billy Crystal introduced the presenter for the Best Picture award.

Rafe and Claire sat with their clasped hands hidden in the folds of her champagne-silver chiffon gown, listening to an aeon's-long three-minute presentation of all the movies that had been nominated for the award that year.

Halfway through the presentation, Rafe leaned over and whispered in his wife's ear. "Are you going to be crushed if *Desperado* doesn't win?"

Claire turned her jewel-bright eyes to his. "Are you?"

"I asked first."

Claire thought about it for a minute. Would she be crushed? After all, she'd accomplished what she'd wanted to accomplish with the movie, and then some. She'd proven herself beyond a shadow of a doubt. Her reputation as a producer in her own right had been established for all time—or until she produced a flop, whichever came first. She had a career as a screenwriter if she wanted it. The funny thing was, it didn't seem to matter nearly as much as it had before. It had stopped mattering so much, she realized, when she'd finally broken free of her past.

It hadn't been her worth as a producer she'd wanted to prove, so much as her worth as a woman. And it was the man sitting beside her who'd shown her that worth, who'd shown her—and continued to show her, every single day—what kind of woman she really was. Warm. Emotional. Capable of loving and being loved.

Oh, the tabloids still called her the Ice Queen, but it didn't bother her anymore because she knew it wasn't true.

"Claire?" Rafe murmured, worried when she took so long to respond.

She smiled into his eyes. "No, I won't be crushed," she assured him. "Disappointed, but not crushed. How 'bout you?"

Rafe grinned. "Hell, yes. I'll be crushed. I'll be *devastated*. You'll have to take me home and do all kinds of lewd and lascivious things to my body to help me get over the trauma of losing."

"Lewd and lascivious, huh? That sounds interesting," she whispered, her body beginning to heat at the thought.

"And the Oscar for Best Picture goes to . . ." The presenter paused to heighten the drama.

Oblivious to the cameras zooming in on them from all over the auditorium in anticipation of capturing their reaction to the announcement of the winner, Claire and Rafe squeezed each other's hands and leaned close to share a loving kiss. Whoever took home the Oscar tonight, they had already won.

And all it had taken was a little push in the right direction.